Infants of the Spring

Infants of the Spring
Wallace Thurman

MINT EDITIONS

Infants of the Spring was first published in 1932

Print ISBN: 9798888970317

E ISBN: 9798888970348

 MINT
EDITIONS

MintEditionBooks.com

Publishing Director: Katie Connolly
Design: Ponderosa Pine Design
Production and Project Management: Micaela Clark
Typesetting: Syd Miles

CONTENTS

I	10
II	19
III	23
IV	27
V	36
VI	43
VII	47
VIII	51
IX	59
X	67
XI	73
XII	82
XIII	90
XIV	93
XV	99
XVI	102
XVII	106

XVIII   111

XVIX   121

XX   136

XXI   145

XXII   158

XXIII   166

XXIV   173

XXV   177

The canker galls the infants of the spring
Too oft before their buttons be disclosed,
And in the morn and liquid dew of youth
Contagious blastments are most imminent.

– Hamlet

The people I am most fond of are those who are not quite achieved,
who are not very wise, a little mad, 'possessed'.

A man slightly possessed is not only more agree able to me; he is
altogether more plausible, more in harmony with the general
tune of life,
a phenomenon unfathomed yet, and fantastic, which makes
it at the same time so confoundedly interesting.

– Maxim Gorky

I

Raymond opened the door with a flourish, pushed the electric switch and preceded his two guests into the dimly illuminated room.

"Here we are, gentlemen."

"Nice diggings you have here," Stephen said.

"Damn right," Raymond agreed. "I'm nuts about 'em. Sam doesn't like my studio, though. He thinks it's decadent."

"I merely objected to some of the decorations, Ray."

"Namely, the red and black draperies, the red and black bed cover, the crimson wicker chairs, the riotous hook rugs, and Paul's erotic drawings. You see, Steve, Sam thinks it's all rather flamboyant and vulgar. He can't forget that he's a Nordic and that I'm a Negro, and according to all the sociology books, my taste is naturally crass and vulgar. I must not go in for loud colors. It's a confession of inferior race heritage. Am I right, Sam?"

"It's all Greek to me anyhow," Stephen murmured. "I like the room. . . and these pictures are rather astonishing. Who did them?"

"The most impossible person in the world," Samuel answered.

"Wrong again," Raymond said. "Paul is one of the most delightful people in the world. I only hope he drops in before you leave, Steve. You'll enjoy meeting him."

"He certainly handles his colors well."

"But his pictures are obscene," Samuel protested. "They are nothing but highly colored phalli."

Raymond shrugged his shoulders.

"You argue with him, Steve. I'm worn to a frazzle trying to make him see the light. Everything that Sam doesn't understand, he labels depraved and de generate. As an old friend, maybe you're willing to take up his education where I'm leaving off. Right now, I'm going to have a highball. Shall I fix three?"

Raymond retired to the alcove addition to his studio, and prepared the three highballs. When he returned to the room, Stephen Jorgenson was minutely examining the various drawings which adorned the wall, while Samuel stood stiffly in front of the false fireplace, patently annoyed by his friend's interest in what he considered obscene trivia.

"I made yours weak, Sam."

"You have educated him, at that," Stephen said. "When he was at the University of Toronto, he wouldn't even take a drop of ale."

"I'm glad I didn't know him then. He's impossible enough now." Raymond smiled maliciously at Samuel, then held his glass aloft.

"Here's to your first time in Harlem, Stephen Jorgenson, to your first day in New York, and to your first visit to these United States. Prosit."

Raymond and Stephen drained their glasses. Samuel sipped a little of the liquid, made a wry face, then placed his glass upon the ledge of the mantlepiece.

"It's funny," Raymond mused, "how things happen. Three hours ago we were total strangers. Twenty-four hours ago we were not even aware of one another's existence. And now, Steve, I feel as if I had known you all of my life. It's strange, too, because the acquaintanceship began under such evil auspices. First of all Samuel introduced us, and I always dislike Samuel's friends. He knows the most godawful people in the world. . . social service workers, reformed socialistic ministers, foreign mis sionaries, caponized radicals, lady versifiers who gush all over the place, Y. M. C. A. secretaries and others of the same dogassed ilk. They are all so saccharine and benevolent. They talk of nothing but service to mankind, not realizing that the greatest service they could render mankind would be self extermination. And you have no idea how they sympathize with me, a poor, benighted Negro.

"Consequently, when I came to dinner tonight, I was prepared to be bored and uncomfortable. Sam had told me nothing except that he had a foreign friend whom he wanted me to meet. And surprisingly enough you were foreign, foreign to everything familiar either to Samuel or myself."

"You were foreign to me, too," Stephen said.

"I know it," Raymond replied. "And you can imagine my surprise to find that you were the uncomfortable one. It rather startled me to find someone usurping my position at one of Samuel's dinners. I didn't know—I still don't know for that matter—what our host had told you about me. And of course I had no idea what you thought or felt about Negroes. I got the impression, though, that you were anticipating some sort of cannibal attack. Actually. The expression on your face as you entered the cafe plainly said: I hope these Negroes find their dinners ample. Otherwise they're liable to pounce upon me."

"Ray!" Samuel exclaimed. There was a note of reproof in his voice, but before he could continue, Stephen spoke:

"By golly, you're right. I was frightened. After all I had never seen a Negro before in my life, that is, not over two or three, and they were only dim, passing shadows with no immediate reality. New York itself was alarming enough, but when I emerged from the subway at 135th Street, I was actually panic stricken. It was the most eerie experience I have ever had. I felt alien, creepy, conspicuous, ashamed. I wanted to camouflage my white skin, and assume some protective coloration. Although, in reality, I suppose no one paid the slightest attention to me, I felt that everyone was sizing me up, regarding me with hostile eyes. It was ghastly. The strange dark faces, the suspicious eyes, the undercurrent of racial antagonism which I felt sweeping around me, the squalid streets, barricaded by grim tenement houses, and then that depressing public dining room in which Samuel and I were the only white persons. I was ready to bolt."

"See, Sam," Raymond said, "how unconsciously cruel you are? Of all the places to bring an innocent foreigner the moment he sets foot in America. Harlem terrifies me, and I've been here long enough to be acclimated, to say nothing of my natural affinity to the place."

"I think Steve's exaggerating."

"Exaggerating my great aunt. I'm guilty of understatement, if anything."

"Certainly," Raymond said. "There are perhaps a dozen or more things you'd like to say about your impressions, but you desist for fear of wounding me. Don't, for God's sake. I'm not the least bit self-conscious about my race. And I prefer brutal frankness to genteel evasion anytime."

Stephen's keen, blue eyes once more regarded the small and slender Negro who sat opposite him, noting the smooth dark skin to which the amber colored bulbs imparted red overtones, and becoming particularly interested in the facial features. They were, Stephen thought, neither Nordic nor Negroid, but rather a happy combination of the two, retaining the slender outlines of the first, and the warm vigor of the second, thus escaping both Nordic rigidity, and African coarseness. Equally as interesting were the eyes. When in repose they seemed to be covered by some muddy mask, which rendered them dull and lifeless. But Stephen had noticed that when Raymond became animated, his eyes shed this mask and became large, brilliant and fiery.

Samuel interrupted his reverie.

"I think it's time we were getting downtown, Steve."

"Why? Have we something else to do? This place is so restful, I don't want to move."

"Stay, then," Raymond said. "Sam's afraid I'll contaminate you if you stay around me too long."

"You're being ridiculous, Ray."

"Tell me," Stephen said. "Do you two always get along so famously?"

"Umhuh," Raymond answered. "We're really quite fond of one another, though. Otherwise I'd never countenance Samuel's Puritanism and spirit of uplift, and I'm sure he'd resent my persistent badgering. We disagree about everything. And yet there are moments when we get great pleasure out of one another's company. I need Sam's steadying influence, and he is energized by what he calls my animalism."

He smiled affectionately at the discomfited Samuel, who

nervously shifted his feet, then turned to the mantelpiece, caught sight of the drink he had forgotten, and once more took the glass in his hand.

"Are you still nursing that?" Raymond asked. "I'm ready for another. How about you, Steve?"

"I can't say that I'm crazy about the taste of gin, but I suppose the effect is desirable." your

"Quite. You must get used to Harlem gin. It's a valuable and ubiquitous commodity. I couldn't do without it."

Raymond once more went into the alcove to refill the empty glasses, his mind busy contrasting the two Nordics who were his guests. Stephen was tall and fashioned like a Viking. His hair, eyes and complexion all testified to his Norse ancestry. Samuel was small, pale, anemic. His hair was blond and his eyes were blue, but neither the blondness nor the blueness were as clearly defined or as positive as Stephen's. Samuel's ancestors had been dipped in the American melting pot, and as a result, the last of the line bore only a faint resemblance to his original progenitors.

"Tell me more about the fellow who drew these," Stephen said as Raymond returned to the room and handed him a full glass of gin and ginger ale.

"Nothing doing," Raymond replied. "Paul's a person you've got to see to appreciate. You wouldn't believe what I could tell you. It's about time he was dropping in. He knew I was going out to dinner tonight. That's why he isn't here now."

"Tell me this, then," Stephen asked, "do all these hideous Harlem houses have such nice interiors?"

"Not by a damn sight. Most of them are worse inside than out. You should see some of the holes I've had to live in. It just happens that my present landlady is a visionary as well as a businesswoman. She has dreams. One of them is that someday she will be a bestselling author. That accounts for this house. She knew the difficulties experienced by Harlem artists and intellectuals in finding congenial living quarters, and reasoned that by turning this house over to Negroes engaged in creative work, she would make money, achieve prestige as a patron, and at the same time profit artistically from the resultant contacts."

"Is the house entirely filled with these. . . er. . . creative spirits?"

"Not yet. But we have hopes. Only the top floor remains in the hands of the Philistines. One of the ladies up there claims to be an actress, but we doubt it, and neither of her two children are precocious. The other tenant on that floor is a mysterious witch-like individual, who was living here when Euphoria leased the house, and who refused to be put out. Pelham, Eustace, Paul, and myself make up the artistic contingent. Wait till you meet the others. They're a rare collection."

Ten minutes later, Paul and Eustace entered the room.

"Oh, hell," Paul said, "another Nordic. Ain't he a beauty, Eustace?"

"Cut the comedy, Paul. I want to introduce you to Stephen Jorgenson. He just arrived in America today, and this is of course his first visit to Harlem. Don't scare him to death. This is Paul, Steve. He's responsible for all these abominable drawings. And this is Eustace Savoy, actor, singer, and what have you. He runs a den of iniquity in the basement, and is also noted for his spoonerisms."

"Mad to gleet you," Eustace said, living up to his reputation.

"Have you ever been seduced?" Paul asked. "Don't blush. You just looked so pure and undefiled that I had to ask that."

Stephen looked inquiringly at Raymond.

"Don't mind Paul. He's harmless."

"I like your drawings," Stephen said.

"You should," Paul replied. "Everybody should. They're works of genius."

"You're as disgusting as ever, Paul."

"I know it, Sam, but therein lies my charm. By the way, how did you ever get to know such a gorgeous man as this. . . you know, Steve," he added abruptly, "you should take that part out of your hair and have it windblown. The hair, not the part. Plastering it down like that destroys the golden glint."

"Oh, I say. . . " Stephen began.

"That's all right. I never charge for expert advice. Where's the gin, Ray?"

"In the alcove, of course."

"But you mustn't dride the hinks," Eustace said.

"You're not at all funny," Samuel muttered.

"I'm sorry, Sam. Wait'll I have a couple of drinks. Then I'll shise and rine."

He and Paul went into the alcove.

Paul was very tall. His face was the color of a bleached saffron leaf. His hair was wiry and untrained. It was his habit not to wear a necktie because he knew that his neck was too well modeled to be hidden from public gaze. He wore no sox either, nor underwear, and those few clothes he did deign to affect were musty and disheveled.

Eustace was a tenor. He was also a gentleman. The word elegant described him perfectly. His every movement was ornate and graceful. He had acquired his physical bearing and mannerisms from mid Victorian matinee idols. No one knew his correct age. His face was lined and drawn. An unidentified scalp disease had rendered him bald on the right side of his head. To cover this mistake of nature, he let the hair on the left side grow long, and combed it sidewise over the top of his head. The effect was both useful and bizarre. Eustace also had a passion for cloisonné bric-a-brac, misty etchings, antique silver pieces, caviar, and rococo jewelry. And his most treasured possession was an onyx ring, the size of a robin's egg, which he wore on his right index finger.

Stephen was frankly bewildered by these two strange beings who had so unceremoniously burst into the room, and forced themselves into the spotlight. Truly, as Raymond had said, this house did harbor a rare collection of individuals.

"I hope you didn't drain the bottle," Raymond said, as Paul and Eustace pranced merrily back into the room, carefully nursing their filled glasses.

"But we thought all of that was for us," Paul said.

"Damned hogs."

"Where did you come from, Steve?" Paul asked.

"Copenhagen, Denmark."

"Oh, that's where they make snuff."

"Snuff?"

"I'm ready to go whenever you are, Steve," Samuel was restless and bored.

"But you can't take him away so soon. I haven't had a chance to talk to him yet," Paul protested. "I've got to tell him about my drawings. He looks like he might have sense enough to appreciate them."

"He's tired, Paul, and once you start to talk, we won't get home tonight."

"But I don't want to go home yet, Sam."

"See there," Paul exclaimed triumphantly, "I knew he had sense. Tell me about yourself, Steve." Paul squatted himself on the floor before Stephen's chair.

"There's nothing to tell. I was born in Canada. My father was Norwegian, my mother was a Dane. I was educated at the University of Toronto where I met Sam and identified myself as much as possible with things American. My folks moved back to Copenhagen. I spent the summer with them, and I'm here now to get a Ph.D. from Columbia."

"Why?"

"Because there's nothing else to do. If I stop going to school, I'll have to work, and the only kind of work I can do is professorial. I don't want to do that, so, as long as the old man foots the bills, I'll stay in school."

"See," Paul exclaimed. "He is one of us."

"God forbid," Samuel said, stifling a yawn.

"Now, Paul, tell me about your drawings."

"That's easy. I'm a genius. I've never had a drawing lesson in my life, and I never intend to take one. I think that Oscar Wilde is the greatest man that ever lived. Huysmans' Des Esseintes is the greatest character in literature, and Baudelaire is the greatest poet. I also like Blake, Dowson, Verlaine, Rimbaud, Poe and Whitman. And of course Whistler, Gauguin, Picasso and Zuloaga."

"But that's not telling me anything about your drawings."

"Unless you're dumber than I think, I've told you all you need to know."

There was a timid knock on the door.

"Come in," Raymond shouted.

Pelham sidled into the room. He was short, fat and black, and was attired in a green smock and a beret which was only two shades darker than his face.

"Hello, everybody." His voice was timid, apologetic. "I didn't know you had company."

"That's all right," Raymond reassured him. "Mr. Jorgenson, this is Pelham Gaylord. He's an artist too,"

"Pleased to meet you," Stephen proffered his hand. Gingerly Pelham pressed it in his own, then quickly, like a small animal at bay, stepped back to the door, and smiled bashfully at all within the room.

"Pelham's the only decent person in the house," Samuel said.

"You mean he's the only one you can impress." It was Paul who spoke. "But I'm tired of sitting here doing nothing. There's no life to this party. We need to celebrate Steve's arrival. We need some liquor. Let's go to a speakeasy."

"Who's going to pay the bill?" Raymond asked.

"Who?" Paul repeated. "Why, Steve of course. It's his celebration, and he's bound to have some money."

"But. . . " Samuel started to protest.

"But hell. . . " Paul interrupted. "Get your hat and coat, Steve. You, too, Ray and Eustace. Let Sam stay here with Pelham. Otherwise he'll spoil the party."

"But suppose I wish to go with you?"

"And leave Pelham alone? Nothing doing, Sam. I'm sure you have lots to say to one another. And Pelham must have written some new poems today. Can't you see the light of creation in his eyes?"

All during this barrage of banter, Paul had been helping first Stephen and then Raymond into their coats. And before there could be further protest, he had ushered Stephen, Eustace and Raymond out of the room, leaving Samuel gaping sillily at the grinning Pelham.

II

S amuel Carter had migrated from a New England college to Greenwich Village intent upon becoming a figure in the radical movement. He had been seduced into radicalism by a Jekyll and Hyde professor of economics, who mouthed platitudes in the classroom, and preached socialism in private seances to a few chosen students. As a rule, these students were carefully chosen. Samuel was one of the professor's mistakes. How they became attracted to one another in the first place is one of those minute, insoluble mysteries which can only be attributed to fate's perversity. However, the fact remains that Samuel became a member of the professor's private lecture group, and was innocently conscripted into the radical movement, although nature had stamped him an indelible conservative.

He had been obsessed, during his first days in New York, with the idea of becoming a martyr. His professor had inflamed his anemic mind with bio graphical yarns of radicals who had sacrificed their lives for their principles. Samuel was going to do likewise. He was going to be a rebellious torchbearer, a persecuted spirit child of Eugene Debs and Emma Goldman, subject to frequent imprisonment, and gradually becoming inured to being put on the rack by the sadistic policemen who upheld the capitalistic regime.

To prepare himself for his future glory, he dived recklessly into the many cross currents of the radical movement. He ultimately allied himself with every existing organization which had the reputation of being red or pink, no matter how disparate their aims and policies. He was thus able to be in sympathy both with anarchists and pacifists, socialists and communists. He went to the aid of any who called, and was unable to understand his universal unpopularity.

But Samuel was not destined to be a martyr or even a leader. He had to content himself with carrying banners in protest parades, or braving a picket line, and being general utility man to the officers and members of all the various organizations to which he belonged. When there were placards or throwaways to be distributed, it was Samuel who did the honors. When there were to be meetings, it was Samuel who arranged for extra chairs, Samuel who provided water for the speakers of the evening, Samuel who was called upon to open windows, find lost articles, and importune the superintendent for more heat. He had become a letter perfect prop man for the theater in which he longed to play a leading role.

Samuel became depressed. And concurrent with the realization that he was and probably would remain a mere nobody in the radical movement, he also became aware of a duality in his nature, a clash between his professed beliefs and his personal sympathies. More often than not he considered his capitalistic opponents in a more favorable light than he did his radical allies. Strikers, paralyzing the efficiency of some commercial machine, became, to Samuel, silly fools who did not know when they were well off. In short, his natural conservatism began to assert itself. It became obvious that he was one of God's elect, and that he would find neither fame nor riches among the disciples of the devil.

Samuel grew restive and resentful. He absented himself from his usual haunts, took to brooding, and was on the verge of crawling penitently back to the wealthy uncle who had offered to set him up in business, when he became aware of a new cause in which he might possibly realize his earlier ambitions. He entered the lists in an arena in which his mediocrity was overlooked because he had a pale face, and because he had assumed the role of a belligerent latter-day abolitionist. He became a white hope, battling for the cause of the American Negro.

No Negro ever had the welfare of his race so much at heart as did the alien Samuel. News of a lynching upset him for days. He would excitedly buttonhole everyone with whom he came into contact, and be apoplectic in his denunciation of lawless southern mobs. Apprised of isolated cases of racial discrimination in restaurants or theaters, Samuel would go into a rage, write letters to all the daily newspapers and to city officials, excoriating the offending management, asking for a general boycott, and demanding police and legislative action.

As a reward for all this vigorous crusading, Samuel soon found himself vociferously acclaimed by Negroes. His mail was tremendous. Grateful darkies from coast to coast sent him letters of appreciation or appeals for help. The Negro press eulogized him both in the news columns and on their editorial pages. Negro leaders were proud to be associated with him, and to grant him any assistance he might need. And what made the role eminently satisfying was the vilification and abuse visited upon him by certain cliques of his fellow whites. At last Samuel had become a martyr.

Raymond and Paul were the only Negroes he knew who openly ridiculed both him and his cause. Despite this, he was attracted to them. After all, they were outstanding personalities, and Samuel felt that it was part of his duty to remain friendly with them. Pelham Gaylord, though, was a Negro who pleased Samuel. Pelham was servile, deferential, and quite impressed by Samuel's noisy if ineffectual crusade. And it soothed Samuel's rankled vanity somewhat to talk to Pelham about his work after the others had so unceremoniously carted Stephen off to a nearby speakeasy. He monopolized the entire conversation, talking about the trials and tribulations of the misunderstood and mistreated Negro, and out lining what he intended to do about it. His monologue was ended only by the boisterous reentry of the four truants.

"So here you are," Paul shouted, "in dear old Pelham's atelier. How do you like his new poems?"

"He ain't heard 'em yet," Pelham said as he busied himself taking Stephen's coat and hat.

"I bet Pelham ain't hadda chance to say one word. Didn't you monopolize the conversation, Sam?" Eustace grinned at the scowling Samuel.

"Steve likes our speakeasy, Sam," Raymond said.

"But not our licker," Eustace added.

"At last I know what firewater is."

"Don't you think we'd better go now?" Samuel asked.

"Pull down your hair, Sam, and be yourself," Paul said. "Steve's just beginning to enjoy himself.

We may go to a cabaret later."

"But. . ."

"Shut up, Sam," Raymond said. "We promised Steve another thrill. He wants to see Pelham's pictures and hear some of his poetry. Get busy, Pelham."

Pelham was flustered but ambitious. He was always childishly eager to exhibit his pictures or to read his poems. With many superfluous hand movements, he pointed to the various pictures on the wall. "That there," he announced proudly, "is a portrait of Paul Robeson. I copied it from a newspaper photograph."

Stephen looked, gaped, then hurriedly shifted his gaze. His face became flushed. His eyes sought the faces of his companions. He could see that, with the exception of Samuel, all were having difficulty sup pressing their laughter. Once more Stephen glanced at the charcoal monstrosity, and then looked ceiling ward as Pelham jauntily pointed out the portrait he had done of Raymond.

III

Stephen had been in New York for a month now, and most of that month had been spent in company with Raymond. Their friendship had become something precious, inviolate and genuine. They had become as intimate in that short period as if they had known one another since childhood. In fact, there was something delightfully naive and childlike about their frankly acknowledged affection for one another. Like children, they seemed to be totally unconscious of their racial difference. It did not matter that Stephen's ancestors were blond Norsemen, steeped in the tradition of the sagas, and that Raymond's ancestors were a motley ensemble without cultural bonds. It made no difference between them that one was black and the other white. There was something deeper than mere surface color which drew them together, something more vital and lasting than the shallow attraction of racial opposites.

Their greatest joy came when they could be alone together and talk. . . talk about any and everything. They seemed to have so much to say to one another, so much that had remained unsaid all of their respective lives because they had never met anyone else with whom they could converse unreservedly. And no matter how often these conversational communings occurred, no matter how long they lasted, there always seemed to be much more to say.

Stephen was absorbed in learning about Harlem and about Negroes. Raymond was intrigued by the virile Icelandic sagas which Stephen read in the original and translated for his benefit. And both of them were eager to air their thoughts about literature. . .

Ulysses was a swamp out of which stray orchids grew. Hemingway exemplified the spirit of the twenties in America more vividly than any other contemporary American novelist. To Raymond, Thomas Mann and André Gide were the only living literary giants. André Gide was not on Stephen's list, but Sigrid Undset was. Neither liked Shaw. They agreed that Dostoievsky was the greatest novelist of all time, but Stephen had only contempt for Marcel Proust whom Raymond swore by, but didn't read. Stendhal, Flaubert and Hardy were discussed amicably, but the sparks flew when they discussed Tolstoi or Zola. And at the mention of Joyce's *Dubliners* and *The Portrait of the Artist as a Young Man* both grew incontinently rhapsodic. "And Hamsun: You mean you haven't read *Hunger*, Ray? God's teeth, man, that's literature."

Their likes and dislikes in literature were sufficiently similar to give them similar philosophies about life, and sufficiently dissimilar to provide food for animated discussions. It was only when their talk veered to Harlem that they found themselves sitting at opposite poles.

Raymond prided himself on knowing all the ins and outs of Harlem. He had been resident there for over three years, during which time he had explored every nook and cranny of that phenomenal Negro settlement. It had, during this period, attained international fame, deservedly, Raymond thought. But he was disgusted with the way everyone sought to romanticize Harlem and Harlem Negroes. And it annoyed him considerably when Stephen began to do likewise. Together they had returned to the spots which Raymond had ferreted out before. They visited all of the cabarets, the speakeasies, the private clubs, the theaters, the back street rendezvous. Stephen was uncritical in his admiration for everything Negroid that he saw. All of the entertainers, musicians, singers, and actors were. . . marvelous. So were all the other Negroes who seemed to be accomplishing one thing or the other. Stephen, like all other whites who had only a book knowledge of Negroes, seemed surprised that a people who had so long been enslaved, and so recently freed, could make such progress. Raymond tried to explain to Stephen that there was nothing miraculous about the matter.

"Can't you understand, Steve," he would say, "that the Negro had to make what progress he has made or else he wouldn't have survived? He's merely tried to keep the pace set by his environment. People rave about the progress of the Negro. It is nothing near as remarkable, that is generally, as the progress made by foreign immigrants who also come to this country to find freedom from a state of serfdom and illiteracy just as stringent as that of the pre-and post-Civil War Negro. And as for Harlem. It's bound to be a startling and wondrous community. Is it not part and parcel of the greatest city in the world? Is it any more remarkable than the Ghetto or Chinatown or the Bronx? It has the same percentage of poverty, middle class endeavor, family life, and underworld, functioning under the same conditions which makes city life a nightmare to any group which is economically insecure. New York is a world within itself, and every new portion of it which gets discovered by the sophisticates and holds the spotlight, seems more unusual than that which has been discovered before."

"Jesus Christ, Ray, you don't appreciate the place. You're too much a part of it."

"Me a part of Harlem? How come?"

"You know what I mean."

"But I don't."

"Well, you live here. You've always lived here."

"Three years isn't always, Steve, even though it may seem like a lifetime."

"You're quibbling now."

"I'm not quibbling. The fault lies with you. Just because you've overcome your initial fear of the place and become fascinated by a new and bizarre environment, should you lose your reason? Harlem is New York. Please don't let the fact that it's black New York obscure your vision."

"You're both cynical and silly."

"Granted. But if you had lived in Harlem as long as I have, you would realize that Negroes are much like any other human beings. They have the same social, physical and intellectual divisions. You're only being intrigued, as I have said before, by the newness of the thing. You should live here a while."

"That's just what I'd like to do."

"Well. . . why not?"

"By jove, that's an idea. I'll move in with you."

"Move in with me?"

"Sure. I much prefer this room to the one I have now, and certainly prefer your company to that of those nincompoops at the International House."

"White people don't live in Harlem."

"Why not?"

"It just isn't done, that's all. What would your friends say?"

"You're the only friend I give a damn about. If you want me, I don't see why I shouldn't live here."

"There isn't any reason why you shouldn't, but. . . "

"But hell, I'm moving in tomorrow. O. K.?"

"I'll be damn glad to have you, Steve."

Twenty-four hours later, Stephen had moved to Harlem.

WALLACE THURMAN

IV

There were four people in Eustace's basement studio. All held glasses in their hands, glasses containing gin and ginger ale.

"We've got a name for the house," Eustace announced as Stephen and Raymond entered.

"What is it?" Stephen asked.

"Niggeratti Manor."

"Whose idea was that?"

"Paul's, of course."

"Niggeratti Manor," Stephen repeated. "I don't quite get it."

"You wouldn't, Steve."

"All of us can't be as clever as you, Paul."

"I bet Ray gets it…don't you?"

"Niggeratti Manor… hmmm… quite appropriate, I would say. God knows we're ratty enough."

"Here's your drinks."

Pelham handed both the newcomers a ginger ale highball.

"But how does Steve fit into that?"

"Easy enough, Eustace. Isn't he Raymond's roommate?"

"Are you really going to *live* in Harlem, Steve?"

Samuel inquired incredulously.

"Certainly. Why not?"

"Oh, nothing. Naturally, I'm surprised."

"You mustn't let so many things surprise you, Sam. It's a sign of adolescence."

"As you were told before, Paul… "

"Yes, I know everyone can't be as clever as I am, but for one who is so frequently among clever people, you are one dumb white man."

Everyone laughed except Samuel, whose lean, pale face became suffused with pink.

"Where are the girls?"

"Who wants to know?"

"Who in the hell asked?"

"You, Ray."

"Fiderk you, Paul. I'm not Sam, you know."

"O. K., Colonel."

There was a knock on the window. It was the usual signal. Pelham rushed to the outside door. He was heard greeting Bull, who almost immediately strode into the room.

"Everybody sober?" he inquired.

"I should hope to tell you. It's obscene for artists to get drunk before midnight."

"Cut the highbrow stuff, Paul. Gimme a drink, Pelham. There's another quart in my overcoat pocket."

"Hooray for Bull." Eustace, the host, pulled the cord of his ubiquitous green dressing gown tighter around his waist, and made a curtsey. Bull made an awkward attempt to reciprocate, but his clumsy, bulky body did not respond gracefully. For Bull was the personification of what the newspaper headlines are pleased to call a burly Negro. He was short for his weight and his head nestled close to broad. shoulders. His physique was not attractive, but it exuded strength and vitality, and made everyone else in the room appear to be puny, inferior.

Pelham passed a round of drinks. As he was doing this there was another knock on the window.

"Must be the girls," Ray surmised.

Pelham set his tray down and hastened to the outside door.

"Handy guy, Pelham."

"I'll say he is."

"Old housemaid right down to the bricks," Eustace declared in a laugh-provoking falsetto voice.

Pelham ushered two girls into the room. One was quite fair. Under the soft light she could easily have passed for white. Her eyes and hair were a soft pastel brown and her skin was delicately tinted with ivory. Her companion was the color of a roasted chestnut. Her hair was coarse and plentiful and black like her eyes, which were set deep in oversized sockets. There was something stately in the way she carried herself. Raymond had called her a nut brown Juno. Her name was Janet. The other was called Aline.

"Hi."

"Hi yourself."

"Rest your coats and get a drink."

They removed their wraps and went around the room, kissing everyone affectionately. Pelham recovered his tray and continued the serving of drinks, mixing two more for the newcomers.

All were now comfortably settled. The two girls shared the daybed with Stephen. Paul sat on a pillow at their feet. Samuel remained erect in a Windsor chair. Bull sank into the cushioned depths of a Cogswell. Raymond and Eustace occupied the piano bench. Pelham remained standing, the better to resume his bartending activities.

"Well, what's the dirt?"

"No dirt at all, 'cept Steve's permanently become a nigger."

"Paul!" Raymond remembered something Steve had said earlier in the evening.

"To say nigger in the presence of a white person. . . " Perhaps Stephen had been right in his analysis of Paul. He observed him now, sitting tailor fashion on the floor, his six foot body, graceful and magnetic, his dirty yellow face aglow with some inner incandescence, his short stubborn hair defiantly disarrayed, his open shirt collar forming a dirty and inadequate frame for his classically curved neck. He was telling about his latest vagabond adventure. His voice was soft toned and melodious. His slender hands and long fingers described graceful curves in the air. As usual when he spoke, everyone remained silent and listened intently as if hypnotized.

"I was sleepy. Had been walking miles, it seemed, not having any carfare. Somehow or other I didn't want to come home either. Homes are boring places when you don't feel homey. It's nicer just to drop in any place. Well, I saw this apartment house. The lobby was dimly lit. It looked warm and inviting. I went exploring and sure enough there was the nicest little cubby hole beneath the stairs. I lay down and went to sleep. I was dreaming. . . a poignant, excruciatingly beautiful dream. I was in a flower gar den, canopied by spreading oaks, and perfumed by fresh magnolia blossoms. The soil was pungent and black. An assortment of rarely beautiful flowers formed a many colored blanket. White lilies, red lilies, pale narcissi, slender orchids, polychromatic pansies, jaundiced daffodils, soporific lotus blossoms. I was in Eden. The trees were thickly foliaged and only an occasional sunbeam filtered through. Above my head a bevy of full throated thrush caroled sweetly, insinuatingly. I lay down. Then I became aware of a presence. An ivory body exuding some exotic perfume. Beauty dimmed my eyes. The physical nearness of that invisible presence called to me, lured me closer. And as I crept nearer, the perfume pervaded my nostrils, inflamed my senses, anesthetized my brain. My hand reached out and clutched a silken forelock. Involuntarily my eyes closed and I was conscious of being sucked into it until there was a complete merging. For one brief moment I experienced supreme ecstasy. Then the garden disappeared. A harsh voice rasped into my ears. I heard the shrill scream of a frightened woman. I was awake. I had been discovered. I could hear the woman clattering down the tiled hallway, shouting for a policeman. I jumped up, bumped my head against the ascending bottom of the staircase, rushed out into the open spaces of the hallway and saw the woman out on the sidewalk excitedly gesticulating. Up the stairs I ran, cursing her for having spoiled my dream. I reached the roof, crossed over to the next apartment house, came down the stairs, nonchalantly strolled into the street and finally reached home, still lamenting the interruption of my exquisite idyl."

His eyes appraised his audience and were pleased by what they saw. But he had forgotten the prosaic presence of Samuel.

"Did you really have that dream?"

"*You* would ask that."

"That's no answer. Did you really have that dream?"

"Of course."

"Was the presence male or female?"

"I don't know."

For a moment Samuel was uncertain which fork of the road to follow. But he was determined to corner his quarry. With New England thoroughness he continued:

"Did you ever have an affair with a woman?"

"Certainly."

"Did you ever. . ." he lowered his voice, "indulge in homosexuality?"

"Certainly."

Samuel turned red. The others in the room tried no longer to restrain their laughter. It seemed as if the pursued was about to elude the pursuer once and for all. But Samuel was primed for the chase.

"Which did you prefer?" He smiled to himself. Now he had him. Surrender was inevitable. His eyes prematurely evinced the light of victory. Prematurely, because Paul found the one available loophole. With a toss of his head, he quickly replied:

"I really don't know. After all there are no sexes, only sex majorities, and the primary function of the sex act is enjoyment. Therefore I enjoyed one experience as much as the other."

When the laughter had subsided, Pelham passed another round of drinks. These were gulped down quickly and there were cries for more. Pelham grinningly obliged, happy, as always, to be of service. Finally, he had to announce that all of the gin bottles were empty. Eustace jumped to his feet.

"Never no that. Here. . . " He snatched a hat from the top of the piano. "Give till it hurts."

He passed the hat to everyone in the room. The two girls deposited twenty-five cents apiece. Samuel contributed a crushed dollar bill. Bull and Stephen each added another dollar to this. The rest merely passed their hands over the surface of the hat. They were broke.

Eustace counted the money and handed it to Pelham, who immediately left for the corner speak easy.

"I don't know what we'd do without Pelham."

"I think it's a damn shame the way you guys do him."

"He enjoys it, Bull. That's all he's used to, waiting on someone else. His artistic impulses really lie in that direction."

"I don't agree with you, Ray."

"Samuel, you never agree with anyone."

"I was talking to Ray, Paul."

"Why don't you agree? You really can't believe that he has any talent? You've seen his pictures and read his poems." Raymond chuckled to himself as he said this.

"Nevertheless he's a human being and should be treated as an equal. You people make a slave of him."

"I grant you that. But it's of his own making. He gets more pleasure out of waiting on us than he does in painting our portraits. We submit to both, and I warrant he's happier than any of us. Don't you see, Samuel, that your socialistic theories won't work? Treat Pelham as an equal and he would be perfectly miserable. Allow him to do our cooking, washing and ironing and he is happy. He's just a born domestic."

"I still don't agree. You take advantage of his weakness. How can you Negroes expect to better your lot when you are always subjugating a member of your own race?"

"You're all cockeyed, Sam." Stephen spoke for the first time.

"Ain't it the truth." Paul grinned at his perennial adversary. "All humans are equal."

"The more you reiterate that, the less I believe you believe it."

"Oh, shut up, Ray, and you too, Sam. This is no time to argue. I want to dance. Play something, Eustace."

Eustace reluctantly complied with Aline's request.

He seldom played jazz but he had learned one or two numbers in order to accommodate his friends when no other pianist was present. Aline danced with Stephen with whom she had been holding hands and conversing privately all the evening. Raymond danced with Janet. Bull sat down beside Eustace on the piano bench. Samuel remained rooted to his upright Windsor chair.

Before the dance was finished, there was a knock on the window. Bull went to the door and admitted Euphoria Blake. She came bustling into the room, a butterscotch colored bundle of energy.

"Hello, everybody. Good God! Another party?"

"Not at all, landlady mia, just a recreation period."

"Got anything to drink?"

"Not yet, but it will be here soon.

She sat down on the daybed.

"Well, Paul, you gotta job?"

"Of course not."

"Well, why haven't you?"

"I'm waiting for you to find me one." "Be at my office at nine in the morning. And I mean nine. You ought to be ashamed to sponge off your friends all the time."

"*I* should be ashamed? You mean *they* should be honored."

While Euphoria continued her scolding of Paul, Samuel beckoned for Stephen to follow him out of the room. Surprised at the gesture, Stephen disengaged himself from Aline's encircling arm, and reluctantly sauntered out into the hallway. Samuel was leaning against the wall, nervously puffing on a cigarette.

"What's up, Sam?" Stephen asked as he closed the door.

"I'm worried about you."

"About me. . . ?" Stephen laughed. "As Paul would say— How come?"

"Well. . . you're moving up here and all. Is it just the best step to take?"

"Why not? I'm among friends."

"But they're well, you know. . . seems strange for a white man, a respectable white man, to be here in Harlem."

"I don't see it, Sam. Furthermore, don't you preach social equality?"

"Certainly but..

"Well," Stephen interrupted grimly, "I'm only practicing what you profess to believe. Don't be alarmed. I've never been more contented in my life. This is heaven compared to that sterilized joint you put me in."

"I guess it's all right, Steve. . . but. . . you have to be careful."

"About what?"

"About. . . well. . . women."

"Oh, I see. That's what's bothering you, huh, me and Aline. Don't worry, old man, it's just a little flirtation. I have no intention as yet of adding to the current mulatto crop."

"But it's risky, Steve. You see you don't know Negroes, you don't know anything about their peculiar problems."

"I know enough to realize that most of these peculiar problems exist in the minds of people like yourself."

"You're quoting Ray now."

"And I couldn't quote a more sane person. Get this straight, Sam, I'm no hypocrite. I like Ray. I like his friends. I like Aline. . . and none of my likes are based on color. I know nothing about your damn American prejudices, except what I've read in books and been told. A person is a person to me, and I'm well able to choose my own friends."

"There's no need to be angry."

"I'm not angry, Sam, just a little annoyed. You see, I haven't much patience with people who don't have the courage of their convictions."

"But. . . "

Pelham rushed into the hallway from the street, carrying three quarts of gin and several bottles of ginger ale. Stephen opened the door to Eustace's studio, and followed Pelham into the room, leaving Samuel standing in the hallway. Raymond had noticed the unexplained absence and looked inquiringly at Stephen as he reseated himself beside Aline. Stephen caught Raymond's eye and winked just as Samuel, too, decided to rejoin the party.

Pelham was vociferously welcomed, and within a very few moments, had served another round of drinks. Euphoria emptied her glass more quickly than the others, then announced her intention of leaving.

"What's the rush? Don't you like your tenants?" Raymond inquired.

"Better have another drink."

"No thanks, Eustace, I gotta go. It's late, and I have to make time in the morning. Not being an artist. . . yet. . . I must work."

"Why work when you can hire help?" Paul inquired.

"I'm working to make money for myself. . . not for others."

"Materialism personified," Stephen murmured.

"We should ex-communicate you."

"Can't, Paul. We all owe her rent," Raymond said.

"Why bring that up?" Eustace asked mournfully. "Give me another drink, Pelham. Help me drown my sorrows."

"Don't forget me," Aline cried.

"Nor me."

"Or me."

"All of us, damn it."

Pelham whirled around busily. "Come, walk me home, will you, Ray? I've got a wad of bills and I don't like these Harlem streets at night."

"O. K., Euphoria. See you later, gang."

Raymond and Euphoria left the room.

V

After Raymond had gone to his studio and put on his hat and coat, he and Euphoria began the short walk to her own private home.

"Think the house is going to go, Ray?"

"Sure. It's the grandest project, ever."

"It doesn't pay. . . "

"Did you expect it to?"

"I at least expected to collect the rent that's due when it's due."

"Who's behind?"

"Eustace and Pelham. I don't mind about Pelham so much. As long as he's there, I don't have to hire someone to clean the halls or keep the rooms clean or run the furnace. He earns his rent, but Eustace calmly goes on and makes no effort to get hold of money."

"He manages to pick up a few pennies now and then. And he has so much darn junk that he can pawn, that you needn't worry."

"I guess you're right, but I wonder if the house is going to be productive artistically. None of you seem to be doing much work. All I run into are gin parties."

"That's part of our creativeness."

"And I don't think you ought to let Paul hang around there. He's nothing but a parasite."

"I know it, Euphoria. But he's a most charming parasite, and I'm certain he has more talent than any of us."

"Why doesn't he do something with it then?"

"He's got to be awakened, Euphoria. Give him time. He's still very young. Some day he will surprise us all."

"I hope so, but I don't like unproductive people. Those girls, for instance. They're no good."

"They're decorative," Raymond said.

"Nigger girls ain't got no business being decorative unless it's going to bring them in some coin. They're nothing but chippies. I'm sure they'd sleep with anybody. Look how Aline's playing with Stephen. She's just like her mother. I know the old lady well. She passes for white most of the time and lays up with all the cheap Jews she can find. There's one she's been living with for the past three years. Spending her nights with him while her darky husband works and her daughter chases the streets."

"At least everybody is satisfied."

"That's the trouble with Negroes. They're too easily satisfied."

"Everyone can't be as energetic as you, Euphoria."

"Maybe not, Ray, but I want that house back there to be a monument to the New Negro. I wish some of the other artists and writers would move in. And I wish they would all work like Pelham does."

"You should be thankful that there is only one Pelham in the house. . . Now don't start preaching to me about the virtue of his persistence. I know all that. But if this Negro renaissance is going to actually live up to its name and reputation, it's going to be Paul's we need, not Pelham's. We have too many of them now. . . too many like both him and Eustace, striving to make a place for themselves in a milieu to which they are completely alien."

"But Ray. . . Euphoria was amazed at his vehemence."

"That's all right," he interrupted. "You're a grand landlady. No one else in Harlem would stand for any of us, that is, not collectively." They had reached her house. "Here you are, with your wad of bills safe. Drop in and see us tomorrow. Maybe somebody will be working for a change. Good night."

He turned and quickly retraced his steps, thinking of what Euphoria had said about the lack of work being done in Niggeratti Manor, and also remembering a conversation which he and Stephen had had earlier that evening. Stephen had asked:

"Just when are you going to begin work on your novel, Ray?"

"I don't know, Steve," Raymond had answered. "I can't get

started. Something holds me back."

"Laziness?"

"Partially."

"Lack of material?"

"You know it isn't that. Haven't I often outlined the thing for you? I know what I want to write. . . but. . . " He had shrugged his shoulders. "Something holds me back."

Stephen had shifted his gaze and lit a cigarette.

"Are you afraid," he had asked, "of exposing your own peculiar complex?"

"Complex? I have none."

"The hell you haven't," Stephen had said emphatically. "Remember our talk a month ago? You pronounced yourself a Nietzschean. I pronounced you a liar. I still admit I'm at sea. I don't know whether you are or not."

"Neither do I," Raymond had admitted after a moment's pause.

"Which is just what I thought," Stephen had continued. "You'd like to be. You try hard to be. But after all, something holds you back and that same something hinders your writing."

"Why not elucidate?"

"I can't, Ray. You baffle me. Were you like Paul or Eustace or Pelham, I could analyze you immediately. Paul has never recovered from the shock of realizing that no matter how bizarre a personality he may develop, he will still be a Negro, subject to snubs from certain ignorant people. The fact distresses him, although he should ignore both it and the people who might be guilty of such snubs. He sits around helpless, possessed of great talent, doing nothing, wishing he were white, courting the bizarre, anxious to be exploited in the public prints as a notorious character. Being a Negro, he feels that his chances for excessive notoriety à la Wilde are slim. Thus the exaggerated poses and extreme manner isms. Since he can't be white, he will be a most unusual Negro. To say 'nigger' in the presence of a white person warms the cockles of his heart. It's just a symptom of some deep set disease. You're not like that; nor are you like some of the others I've met who are so conscientiously Negroid. Like Pelham for instance, who is a natural born menial with all a menial's respect for his superiors. Or like Eustace who is ashamed of his color, and won't sing spirituals because he does not care to remind the world that he is a Negro and that his ancestors were slaves of whom he is now ashamed."

"Jesus no, Steve, you know I'm not like that. I'm just indifferent to it all. Race to me. . . "

"Yes, race to you," Stephen had interrupted impatiently, "means nothing. You stand on a peak alone, superior, nonchalant, unconcerned. I know all that. You've said it enough. Propagandists you despise. Illusions about Negroes you have none. Your only plea is that they accept themselves and be accepted by others as human beings. But what the hell does it all mean, after all? You claim to have no especial love for your race. You also claim not to despise them. The spectacle of your friends striving to be what they are not, and taking no note of their limitations, sickens you, nay revolts and angers you. Yet you, like the rest, sit about and do nothing. Are you as emancipated as you claim? Aren't you, too, hindered by some racial complex?"

"Nonsense, Steve. I know I'm a Negro and so does everyone else. I certainly cannot pass nor can I effect a change. Why worry about it? I rather love myself as I am, and am quite certain that I have as much chance to make good as anyone else, regardless of my color. In fact, I might even say that being black gives me a certain advantage which a white person of equal talent would be denied."

"Oh, I see."

"You see what?"

"Oh, nothing, let's beat it downstairs." And with this Stephen had terminated the conversation and the two of them had joined the crowd, gathered in Eustace's studio.

Raymond wondered about it now, and also about what Euphoria had said concerning the lack of creative work among Negro artists. Pelham and Eustace of course were not to be considered. They had nothing to contribute anyhow. But Paul and, he thought, himself, did have something to contribute once they made up their minds to do some actual work.

There had been throughout the nation an announcement of a Negro renaissance. The American Negro, it seemed, was entering a new phase in his development. He was about to become an important factor in the artistic life of the United States. As the middle westerner and the southerner had found indigenous expression, so was the Negro developing his own literary spokesmen.

Word had been flashed through the nation about this new phenomenon. Novels, plays, and poems by and about Negroes were being deliriously acclaimed and patronized. Blues shouters, tap dancers, high yaller chorus girls, and singers of Negro spirituals were reaping much publicity and no little money from the unexpected harvest. And yet the more discerning were becoming more and more aware that nothing, or at least very little, was being done to substantiate the current fad, to make it the foundation for something truly epochal. For the time being, the Negro was more in evidence in the high places than ever before in his American career, but unless, or so it seemed to Raymond, he, Paul and others of the group who had climbed aboard the bandwagon actually began to do something worthwhile, there would be little chance of their being permanently established. He wondered what accounted for the fact that most Negroes of talent were wont to make one splurge, then sink into oblivion. Was it all the result, as Stephen had intimated, of some deep rooted complex? Or was it merely indicative of a lack of talent?

Arriving home, Raymond decided to go to his studio before returning to the party in the basement. He could hear laughter and the clink of glasses as he climbed the stairs. On reaching his landing, he was surprised to see rays of light gleaming through the cracks in his studio door. He was certain he had turned out the lights before he had gone out with Euphoria. Perhaps Stephen was there. He hoped so. This would be a propitious time to thrash out certain problems which were tantalizing his mind.

As he turned the knob, he heard a scream. Startled, he hurriedly opened the door, and entered the room. Aline lay on his daybed sobbing. Stephen and Bull, in the center of the room, were locked together, wrestling. Both were quite drunk. Both were swearing breathlessly. Tears were streaming down Bull's virile, scarred face.

"What the hell?" Raymond shouted.

"The bastard's trying to kill me." Stephen was red-faced and panting. Bull was weak with rage. Raymond had little trouble pushing them apart. Stephen collapsed into a nearby chair. Aline struggled to her feet and staggered toward Raymond.

"He slapped me," she screamed.

"An' by God, I'll slap you again." Bull started toward her. She backed away, collided with the daybed, and fell prostrate upon it. Raymond tried to push Bull from the room. Then he noticed that the doorway was filled with a staring mob, inane, drunken, and stupefied by the surprising scene which confronted them. The screams had penetrated to the floor beneath and mounted above the sounds of revelry there.

As Raymond relaxed, Bull regained his strength, thrust Raymond aside, and with fists clenched, face wet and distorted, turned upon the frightened Aline:

"Y' hussy. With a white man, eh? Yer own race ain't good enough? You want a white man? You goddam bitch, I'll kill you."

He made a rush for the figure lying on the daybed. Aline, seeing him come toward her, struggled to her feet, attempted to run, became entangled in the rug and fell heavily to the floor. Stephen snored in his chair. Raymond again threw himself into Bull's way only to be sent crashing into the corner. by the door. His head struck the wall and he was only dimly conscious of the sound of scuffling feet as the rest of the crowd surged into the room. A short struggle ensued. Raymond recovered his balance, and toward the prostrate Aline just as Bull was being forced down the stairs, hysterically raving, blasphemous.

VI

It was noon before Raymond awoke. Stephen was still asleep beside him. Paul lay stretched on the floor indolently smoking a cigarette. He smiled as Raymond sat up in the bed.

"Good morning."

"How in the hell did you get here?"

"I had to sleep somewhere."

Stephen awoke, turned over and blinked, then drew himself into a sitting posture.

"You will seduce colored ladies, will you?" Paul drawled between puffs of smoke.

"Say, was that guy nuts?"

"Oh, no," Paul assured him, "he's just a good Negro."

"You mean he's a damn fool," Raymond interjected angrily.

"For trying folk? To protect the chastity of his women-folk?"

"Go to hell, Paul."

"All right, Ray. But you know I'm right. All niggers can't be as civilized as you."

"Do you mean that guy actually got *sore* at me?"

"Oh, no! He just felt playful." Paul laughed. "Forget it, Steve. I'm going to see how near Pelham has breakfast ready."

When he had gone, Raymond turned to Stephen. "Damn awful mess you started."

"Aw what the hell! You're as bad as Sam. Can't a fellow rush a girl?"

"Certainly."

"Then what's the row about?"

"It's just that all Negroes aren't alike. There are some who quite naturally object to seeing Negro women rushed by white men."

"Horse collar."

"I know it sounds silly to you, but it's true, nevertheless."

"Baloney. Bull was just drunk. Haven't I seen him rush white broads?"

"Certainly. But that's different."

"You're nuts. Let's eat."

He climbed out of the bed and began to dress.

Sullenly, Raymond followed suit. The doorbell rang while they were still at the breakfast table. Pelham with his usual promptitude answered its summons. A moment later he meekly ushered Bull into the kitchen.

"'Lo."

The return greetings were reserved. No one knew just what to say.

"Wha' d' y' say, Steve?" There was a jovial note in Bull's voice as he slapped Stephen on the shoulder. "Weren't we pie-eyed last night? Jeez, I was drunk."

Everyone laughed. There seemed to be nothing else to do. Stephen smiled triumphantly at Raymond. Conversation flourished throughout the rest of the meal and when breakfast was finished, Eustace procured a bottle of gin he had hidden away the night before and led the way to Raymond's studio. Only Pelham remained behind to wash the dishes.

Raymond was intrigued by Bull's attire as he followed him up the stairs. He was clad in a rough-neck sweater and soiled corduroy trousers. On his head was a greasy cap which slithered over his left ear. He was every inch the tough, every inch the cinema conception of a gangster, with one exception. Instead of being fortified with a blackjack or a gun, his left arm was burdened with a mysterious packet of medium sized sheets of cardboard. Eustace mixed the highballs. Soon everyone was comfortably seated, drinking, smoking cigarettes, animated, talkative. Bull alone took little interest in the conversation. He seemed determined to become drunk again, gulping down glass after glass of straight gin, deliberately ignoring the highballs Eustace prepared. His reticence attracted attention. Conversation languished. No one knew what to expect next. Suddenly it came.

"I'm a man, you know."

Only Paul had the temerity to laugh.

"I'm a man. An' I expect to be a man among men. Now

maybe I was in the wrong last night. I'm so goddam bullheaded when I get drunk, but you see," and here he looked directly at Stephen, "I ain't used to seein' no white man with no colored woman. The bastards lynch every nigger that has a white woman and I kinda thinks darkies ought to do the same. But you see, Steve," a note of tenderness crept into his harsh voice, "I forgot you wasn't no ordinary white man. An'. . . " He paused to gulp down another glass of gin. "I'm sorry."

"'S all right, Bull."

Stephen could think of nothing else to say. Raymond and Paul exchanged amused glances. Eustace glided around the room, swishing his green dressing gown, refilling the empty glasses. Meanwhile Bull began orating on race relations. It was impossible for anyone else to get in a word. An uncle his, it seemed, had been lynched on suspicion of having raped a white woman. Although a mere adolescent at the time, Bull had sworn to avenge his kinsman's death by

"Havin' ev'ry white woman I kin get, an' by hurtin' any white man I kin. I hates the bastards. I gets drunk so's I can beat 'em up an' I likes to make their women suffer. But if I ever catch one of the sons of bitches messin' 'round one of my women, hell's doors won't open quick enuff to catch him."

So impassioned did he become that for the moment he once more forgot the alien presence of Stephen. Raymond felt that he should say something, should, perhaps, advance an argument to contravene Bull's point of view. But a realization of how futile anything he might say would prove caused him to hesitate and remain silent. Suddenly Bull began again.

"But, Steve, you're nothin' but a darky like the rest of us. You're a man, see. I like you."

Stephen smiled his thanks. The others grinned mechanically, then busied themselves lighting cigarettes, draining their glasses, clearing their throats, and trying to think of something to say. Paul broke the silence by noticing Bull's packet of cardboard.

"Whatcha got there, Bull?"

"Just some drawin's of mine I brung along to show you."

"Drawings," Paul gasped. Raymond became choked on the gin he was drinking. The others were equally aghast.

"Yeah, I always did like to draw from a kid. Been takin' a correspondence course in commercial art. Ain't like you guys. I'm after money. I don't wanna work for some white man all my life, an' I'm too dumb to be a doctor or anything like that. But I'm apt at drawing."

Tenderly he undid his package, and proudly passed the various sheets of cardboard around the room. On each was a woman, pictured in some situation calculated to illustrate a descriptive pun printed at the bottom of the picture. Every pun included the slogan of some nationally known advertiser. The drawings were painstaking, vigorous and clean cut. Unlike those perpetrated by Pelham, there was some notion of perspective and a pleasing knowledge of human anatomy. But Bull's women were not women at all. They were huge amazons with pugilistic biceps, prominent muscular bulges, and broad shoulders. The only thing feminine about them were the frilled red dresses in which all were attired.

VII

For a week or so after Bull's explosion, things were fairly quiet in Niggeratti Manor. And Raymond had taken advantage of the lull in gin to do some work on the first chapter of his proposed novel. While working on this, he suddenly remembered that it was about time he was getting in touch with Lucille. He telephoned her. She came to the house, but Raymond had a toothache and everyone else had a thirst for liquor. In order to be together alone, they finally made a dinner engagement.

Raymond and Lucille had been pals almost since his first days in Harlem. Raymond had been attracted to her, because she personified what he was wont to call an intelligent woman. And there were few such women, in his opinion, to be found among the Negroes he knew. Their relationship had retained its platonic status only because Lucille had, from the beginning, scorned the suggestion that he should make love to her. At first, it had seemed only natural, in view of their mutual emancipated beliefs, that they should have an affair. Lucille had merely taunted Raymond with doing the conventional male action, once male and female became close friends. Her dissuasion had been subtle and effective, if not entirely sincere. Had Raymond not told her that he believed platonic friendships possible and sensible? He had, and except for infrequent vocal lapses, had seemed content to continue their friendship on that basis.

Recently it seemed as if they were drifting apart. Until the advent of Stephen, Lucille had been Raymond's most intimate companion. They had been constantly together, attending theaters, parties, musicales, and art exhibits. Rarely did two nights pass without their seeing one another, and always had they found it convenient to cancel engagements with other friends, merely to be with one another. There seemed to be no accounting for their present estrangement. Both were conscious of its existence, and both were eager to get together for the first time in over a month in order once more to revive their flagging friendship.

Raymond met her at the subway kiosk at 135th Street and Lenox Avenue. She had come directly uptown from her work as secretary to the publicity. manager of a well-known liberal organization. Her olive brown skin was flushed from the heat and jam of the subway. A stray black curl had escaped from beneath her cloche hat. Her dark, heavily lashed eyes danced merrily. Raymond admired the delicate strength of her trimly clad figure.

"'Lo, 'Cile."

"Hello, Ray. How's the tooth?"

"I've forgotten it."

"Didn't you go back to the dentist?"

"With the tooth not hurting? I should say not."

"Where do we eat?"

"Anywhere but Craig's. Samuel's taking Steve there for dinner. Trying to influence him out of Harlem, I believe."

"Sam is a pill," Lucille said.

"Worse than that. He got all exercised with me last night because I wouldn't attend a meeting of the Brotherhood of Sleeping Car Porters. Accused me of being a self-centered egoist."

"You are."

"I know it, but I'll be damned if I'll join in any crusade to save the Negro masses. I'm only interested in individuals."

"Did you finish your first chapter?"

"Yes, thank God. Sometime this morning after the liquor was gone and I'd kicked Aline and Steve out of my bed."

"Aline and Steve?"

"Umhuh. They're quite gone on one another, despite Bull and Samuel."

"I don't see what Steve sees in her."

"Cat."

"What I really meant, of course, is that I don't see why she wants Steve."

"I thought you liked him."

"I do, Ray, tremendously. He's the only one of your friends I do like without reservation. But I wouldn't go to bed with him."

"He hasn't asked you yet, 'Cile."

"It really wouldn't do him any good if he did. I'd never go to bed with any white man."

"I'm disappointed in you, 'Cile. You, of all people, to talk like that. It's not what you said so much as the implications it carries. You spend ninety-nine percent of your time, in the office and out, with Nordics. You agree with me, ostensibly, that human being is a human being regardless of color. And yet…"

"I wouldn't go to bed with a white man, because I'd never be sure that I wasn't doing it just because he was white."

"Do you think that about Aline?"

"I'd bet my life on it, Ray. And what's more, I'd be willing to bet that almost every other Negro woman Steve meets at your house will automatically assume a horizontal position if he makes the proper passes."

"Oh, shut up, 'Cile."

They were now at 140th Street and Lenox Avenue. Tabb's restaurant confronted them. They entered and descended to the basement grill. Dinner ordered, they settled down to talk.

"How's the job?" Raymond asked.

"Monotonous as ever. I'm damn tired of liberal organizations. I'd like to work for a Babbitt for a change, but Babbitts no like brownskin secretaries."

"Why not try a brownskin Babbitt?"

"I like salary for my work for one thing, and I don't like to do bed duty after hours. Let's don't talk about it. My idea of heaven would be some place where there were no typewriters, adding machines, or sentimental persons prating of creating goodwill between whites and blacks."

"Incidentally. Where is that chap, Miller, who used to work in your office?"

"Gone somewhere to study theology. Came to the conclusion that the only Negroes who could make money and independent were ministers of the gospel. He'll do well, too. He's a dog with the ladies."

"Did he try to make you?"

"I didn't give him the chance."

Raymond looked into her eyes for a moment, then asked abruptly:

"Say, 'Cile, have you ever been in love?"

"Damned tootin! All my life."

"Can't you ever be serious?"

"About love? Not at dinner time. Let's eat."

The waiter had placed their food in front of them. For a moment they both were too busily en gaged eating to talk. Raymond broke the silence.

"How do you like Niggeratti Manor?"

"It's a grand bawdy house. I hope you don't always have a mob like you did the last time I was there. Is Steve going to stay permanently?"

"I hope so."

"Is Aline a part of your plan to keep him there?"

"Don't be silly," Raymond replied indignantly.

"It's all their own doing."

"All right, innocence. But I know you. Half of your life is spent maneuvering your friends."

"Poppycock."

"You're a liar. Why, you'd even make a pawn of me if I'd let you."

"Is that the reason you won't have an affair with me?"

"Affair with you?" Lucille laughed. "Don't be silly."

"I'm not being silly. I'm being quite serious."

"Ray, I've told you dozens of times that you needn't make love to me."

"All right then, let's forget it."

"As you will."

Raymond returned to his food. And he did not notice the contraction of Lucille's eyes, nor the expression of disappointment which flitted across her face, as she realized he had taken her persiflage seriously.

VIII

It was after midnight. Lucille had spent the evening with Raymond, and had just gone home. Everyone else was still congregated in his studio. It had been an evening of sobriety, an evening of serious conversation. And now, with voice low, eyes sullen, Euphoria Blake was telling the story of her life. For a moment she paused, cleared her throat, then clenched her fist and held it against her breast. Her audience was respectful, quiet.

"I went off to school, then. To a little state normal school in the backwoods of Georgia. I had never been away from home before. And my childhood, you know, had been rather lonely. I had never had any friends, never had any comrades but my mother, the dirty little brats she taught, and my father, whom I saw very seldom, because he spent most of his time roaming the highways of Georgia, carrying a guitar, a knapsack and a Bible, preaching to stray groups of peasant Negroes.

"I hadn't wanted to leave home. I did not know how to mix with people, and I was afraid of being called a back number. But I hope you know my mother took no notice of my fear. No siree, she packed me off and I had to seem glad to go.

"Well, I arrived in Huntsville, scared to death. There was to be a bus at the station. I got off the train and looked for it, but couldn't see nothing that looked like a school bus. There didn't seem to be anyone around the station, either. It was so quiet that it was deathlike. I stood there right where I had got off the train, looking silly as hell for a minute, then decided to pass the little shanty which was the station and look around. Maybe the bus was late and would be coming down the road. Well, I looked around. And for looking: Right there on the side of the road near the shanty was a telegraph pole. And dangling from that telegraph pole was the body of a Negro man. He had been lynched.

"I ain't sure what happened after that. I only know I tore lickety split down the road, getting away from that horror just as fast as I could. I ran and ran. Finally some old colored woman hailed me, and from her I found out the way to the school. They hadn't sent the bus, because of the lynching, and everyone was scared to go out.

"Well, I started to school, mechanically going to classes, and having no interest in anything that went on. I stayed to myself as much as possible. I couldn't get the picture of that lynched man out of my mind. It haunted me day and night. I used to have nightmares and holler out loud enough to wake up everybody in the dormitory. The girls used to shun me. The matrons were mean. They said I was kinda queer. I guess I was. My only recreation was to go off in the woods and read. The solitude there sorta pacified me. It was just about this time that I begin to notice copies of *The Crisis* in the school library. From them I learned about the National Association for the Advancement of Colored People. And I also got a crush on Joan of Arc."

She stopped once more. There was fire in her eyes now, and the clenched fist dropped to her lap. A wan smile spread over her face as she continued.

"I was just plain silly, I guess. I don't blame the folks in the school for thinking me crazy. I went to that school for three years and was left absolutely alone. It was only in the woods that I was happy. I went there constantly. They wasn't far from the campus. And no one ever bothered me. By that time I was determined to be a black Joan of Arc, pledged to do something big for my race. I muster make up fiery speeches and shout them out loud to the pine trees. And in my dreams I saw myself on a white charger, leading a black army to victory against white people. The vision sorta got under my skin, and became a sort of motor force, driving me on to do something. I knew no peace. I was impatient for the great day, impatient to become active.

"Negroes had suffered too long. What they needed were leaders who would fight, and fight out in the open. I was to be that leader. I, a mere girl, would show them the way, lead my race over the top. School could hold me no longer. I was going to revolt. I wouldn't be no schoolteacher like my mother, and rot away in some small Southern hole. I wanted to influence a lot of folks."

She paused again. Her tongue coursed slowly over her lips, moistening them. Her eyes no longer flashed fire. The clenched fist once more sought her breast.

"And then," Raymond intoned. He was seated on the floor beside her chair. His eyes hungrily searched her face.

"And then," she repeated before continuing, "I came to New York. I don't know why now. Something just seemed to pull me. I couldn't resist it. There was that vision of Joan of Arc on a white charger. And I had some voices too. Voices which cried: your race needs you. Well, I came to New York. Poor little fool that I was, with no money, no friends, nothing but a bunch of silly dreams, and that terrible urge to fight for my race."

"You were dumb," Paul interjected.

"How do you mean dumb?" Samuel shot back, eager as ever to engage Paul in an argument.

"To be like that. . . to want to fight."

"But man, don't you see she had her race at heart? Haven't you felt a similar urge? I, a white man, have, and all the Negroes I know have, too."

"You haven't known many Negroes, have you Sam?" Paul asked sarcastically.

Samuel was outraged.

"Haven't you any race pride?"

"Fortunately, no," Paul replied coolly. "I don't happen to give a good goddam about any nigger except myself."

Samuel was too flabbergasted to say more. It was incredible that any Negro should make such a statement. Paul was just an unregenerate liar.

"Go on, Euphoria," Raymond urged eagerly. He had no interest in the silly argument between Paul and Samuel. But he did have a vital interest in the tale Euphoria had been telling. Already he saw himself heightening and distilling her story for his own literary use.

Euphoria began speaking again. Her voice was huskier now, and her eyes were not so sullen.

"The moment I got in town, I went to the offices of the National Association for the Advancement of Colored People. It was their pamphlets, you know, and their magazines and speakers which had first aroused me. I knew the whole history of their organization. And I thought they were inspired by the spirit of John Brown. I felt that I had to join them. And that when they heard me talk, saw how eager I was, that they would welcome me with open arms as just the type of woman they had been looking for.

"When I got to their office, I stuttered out to a stenographer the name of the man I wished to see. I had no appointment of course. She suggested that I make one. Then my courage returned. Here, I had come all the way from Georgia, had run off from school, and from my mother. I had tried to make her understand what I wanted to do, and made no impression whatsoever. Never will I forget my last afternoon at home. I had gone to her schoolroom to tell her goodbye. She wouldn't speak to me, but just seemed like she was part of the cold portable blackboard on which she was writing. I had to do something to justify myself, and do it quick.

"Anyhow I got into the inner office. I faced my hero. He was polite but cold. I guess he was tired of dumb darkies busting in on him. His manner froze my courage and left a lump in my throat. I couldn't remember my fiery speeches. My tongue was just like a piece of lead. I could only utter a few silly words. I could only say that I wanted to work. He referred me to the YWCA and politely ushered me out. There really wasn't anything else for him to do, I guess."

"And then. . . " Raymond intoned again, fearful of her pause.

"I was lost. I didn't know what to do. I found the YWCA all right. They gave me a room and found me a job doing housework. Me doing housework when I had come up here to be a race leader. It was both kinda funny and kinda tragic. I couldn't go back home and admit defeat, so I just bided my time, working hard every day, and crying myself to sleep every night. I had lost my forest, my dreams, and my voices. I had nothing left. . . "

She hesitated a moment, asked Raymond for a cigarette, remained immobile while he lit it, then inhaled deeply before she began to talk again.

"I continued to work, and then I started going to Columbia University.

"What did you study?" Raymond interrupted, eager for every detail.

"Economics, Poli Sci, and short story writing. In the daytime I worked in first one kitchen then another. There seemed no escape. Then I met Jane Gray. I was her cook. She was a radical. I was just a cook, until she found me reading Marx. Immediately, I became a new person in her eyes. A being with some intelligence and promise. She talked to me a lot. I told her everything. Gone was the Negro cook. I was a potential radical. Jane Gray then showed me off to all her friends. They made an awful fuss over me a Negro kitchen mechanic who read Marx. I was taken to the Village, and signed into the Socialist Party. Next thing I knew they had me working as an organizer among the foreign women in the needle trades."

She stopped for breath, for she was talking faster now, and her voice was pitched higher.

"At last my dreams had come true. I was not helping just one downtrodden race, but I was helping the entire downtrodden race of working men and working women. It wasn't race prejudice I was fighting now, but capitalism, which I had come to believe was the cause of all prejudice."

"Oh, no," Samuel interrupted hurriedly, eager for another argument. Stephen forestalled him by growling:

"Shut your trap."

Euphoria continued, outwardly oblivious to the trivial interruption.

"See, I was working with women, and through the women I was going to reach the men, and then I was going to help emancipate my men and women by making them all join hands. . . that is, all the workers. It was immense. I was thrilled to death. My old fire returned. Instead of a forest, I now shouted speeches in big, barnlike halls. Instead of birds, I now stilled groups of chattering women, and hushed them with my logic. I lived then. I was happy. In the mornings, I would have conferences with my associates, and draw up campaign plans. In the afternoons, I would tramp from one sweat shop to another. And in the evenings, I would take part in mass meetings and committee caucuses. Then late at night, there would be talk and drink and revelry in cellar cafés down in the Village or in somebody's fire-lit studio. Life became a grand picnic. I soon lost all sight of color and race, so few Negroes did I see. *The Masses* was my Bible. Max Eastman, Floyd Dell, Eugene Debs, and Randolph Bourne were my gods of the day. And then. . . " Her voice became low and steady, "the war came to America. Just like that," she snapped her fingers, "my world went to smash. All my friends who had cursed the capitalist war either joined the army, or else preached patriotism, or allowed themselves to be conscripted. Only a few stood pat and risked going to jail. It seemed as if only my lover and I."

"Your what?" Paul shouted, finally aroused from his lethargy.

"My lover," Euphoria repeated calmly. "I believed in free love, too. You see," she added, almost apologetically, "it was all in the game."

"Was he an o'fay?" Paul queried, glancing significantly at Samuel.

"Yes," she answered quickly, then immediately began talking again as if to ward off further questioning.

"It seemed that change was all around me, but I had no intentions of changing. I kept yelling for peace. I kept on reviling Wilson. I said he had allied himself with the invisible government he had once denounced. I paraded down the sidewalk carrying a plea for peace sign, while soldiers marched down the streets with eyes on the American flag.

I hooted while crowds cheered. And once more I felt so all alone. For a while I remained unmolested. You see," she explained laconically, "everybody thought I was a demented Negro and not to be taken seriously. Had I been white, they would have mobbed me and thrown me in jail long before they did. But my day came too. I was hauled into court and charged with sedition. They had me examined for sanity. They couldn't imagine a Negro being radical. I was found sane of course, but they were lenient with me. They locked me up in the Tombs for three months, and put me to scrubbing floors. My lover brought me food. It was all in the game, and I didn't mind at all."

She stopped again, and relit the cigarette Raymond had given her some time before. During the interval, while she was silently puffing and blowing rings, Paul squirmed closer to her chair, itching to inquire further about the lover. It was the only part of her story in which he was sincerely interested. Raymond was busily preoccupied recapitulating all she had said, making mental notes. Stephen's eyes were fixed on Euphoria's face, and there was admiration in his gaze. Samuel was incredulous and showed it. He was prepared to check up on her story.

He couldn't believe that she could have had such a career as a radical when he had tried so hard to do likewise, and ended up a mere handy man. Furthermore, there was no precedent in his knowledge of Negroes for a woman like Euphoria. Frankly, he didn't believe ninety per cent of what she had said. Suddenly Euphoria dropped her cigarette into an ash tray and began speaking again.

"When they let me out of jail, I quickly returned to my old haunts eager to carry on. I found nothing but strangers. The witch hunters had dissipated the ranks of the reds. All of them who hadn't become patriots were hiding in attics or basements, and muttering their speeches of dissension among themselves. Cowardice and conformatism ruled. I was disgusted as hell. I came back to Harlem. I didn't care any longer about movements of any kind. I became hard and cold like my mother. I had finally lost the troubadour spirit of my father. I opened an employment agency. I began to exploit the people I had once planned to help. I didn't care any longer. I wanted money and nothing else. Harlem offered it. Niggers were coming in by the thousands. They needed homes, and jobs, and there were people who had these homes and jobs to pass around. I began to play with both sides, getting money from all of them, those who needed, and those who had, the employer and the job seeker, the landlord and the tenant. They all came to me and they all paid.

"Occasionally I wandered back to the Village. My friends were all out in the open now, but they were hopelessly divided and utterly changed. I couldn't become interested in any of their programs. I had lost the spark. It has never returned. I only wanted money, because it seemed to me, and still does, that only with money can Negroes ever purchase complete freedom. With money and with art. That's the reason I started this house. And when I get enough money to retire then I'm going to give my time to writing and show the world that I can master the only things in life worth mastering."

The clenched fist relaxed. Her hands clasped in her lap. A smile illuminated her round, butterscotch face as she looked from one to the other of her audience. She was very pleased with herself, and with her story, her story which she had told many times, and which she had embellished with gestures and rhetorical ornamentation. Her eyes were afire. A twisted lace handkerchief unfurled in her lap.

"And your lover?" Paul had finally seized an opportune moment.

"Damn the lover," Stephen interjected. "Here's two dollars. Go get some gin."

IX

Raymond was in his room alone, trying to write a book review, which was already three days overdue. He had purposely delayed beginning the review until he should be in a particularly uncongenial mood. The book was by a Negro and about Negroes. Its author was a woman who, had she been white and unknown, would never have been able to get her book published. It was a silly tale, sophomoric and uninspired. Raymond was pleased with the sarcastic jibes he had summoned to include in the review. He was tired of Negro writers who had nothing to say, and who only wrote because they were literate and felt they should apprise white humanity of the better classes among Negro humanity.

He had just about finished when there was a tap on his door. He had not wished to be disturbed and had so warned everyone in the house. His "come in" was harsh and uninviting. And his frown deepened when he saw that the intruder was Janet. She and Aline were always butting in at the wrong time. He was sorry now that he was responsible for their almost continual presence in Niggeratti Manor. They were decorative and they did liven up parties, but there was no reason why they should make this house their second home.

"Well?"

"Got anything to drink?"

"Is that the reason you disturbed me? No, I have nothing to drink and no money. Isn't there any downstairs?"

"No. Pretty tough, eh?"

"Probably a blessing."

"What's wrong with you?"

"I happen to be busy. Shut up a minute, will you?"

He returned to his writing. Janet meekly curled herself into one of the wicker chairs, and silently puffed away on a cigarette.

Finally Raymond finished. With a grin of satisfaction, he

piled the sheets together. "Finished?"

"Looks like it."

"Don't be so nasty, Ray."

This was said so piteously, so abjectly, that Raymond looked up for the first time and observed her closely. Her eyes were full of tears, and the reddish brown powder, which she used to heighten her own complexion, was streaked with tear lanes.

"What the hell?"

"I'm a damn fool, Ray."

"So are we all."

Janet wiped her eyes, then daubed her face with a russet powder puff. This done, she rummaged in her purse for another cigarette.

"Ray. . . I'm in love."

"Poppycock."

"Honest to God."

"With whom?"

"Steve."

Raymond smiled in spite of himself.

"Don't be funny."

"I ain't, Ray. I love him, an'. . ."

"So does your best friend."

"You think she does?"

"Well, she acts like it." He was bored now and anxious for solitude, for he wished to mull over and revise what he had written.

"She don't love him, Ray. She just took him to show me she had more chance."

"Oh, yeah."

"But don't you see, Ray," her voice was thick and her words hurried, passionate, "if he'd never seen her I'd a had him. He likes her best 'cause she's almost white. All white men are that way. They'll pass up a brown girl to get to a high yaller."

"You're a bigger fool than I thought you were."

"It's serious, Ray. I never fell for a white man before. Aline has. But Steve's the first one for me and I'd give anything to have him."

"Just because he's white?" He remembered Lucille's similar assertion. His words were sharp and scornful.

"It's not that, Ray." She was trying hard to make him understand. "It's just that... it's just that he's different."

"Different from Negroes. He has a white skin. It's a badge of honor you'd like to wear. Jesus, are you Negro women as bad as Negro men?"

The tears receded. The eyes flashed angrily.

"I don't see where you got any right to talk. What about Barbara... She's not white, I suppose?"

"Well, what about her? We're good friends, yes."

"Good friends, yeah, I know. So are Steve and Aline good friends. The little whore. But I'll show her. She can't keep him. I ain't yaller, but I can get a white man the same as she."

Abruptly she paced out of the room and slammed the door behind her. For a moment Raymond was utterly flabbergasted. The whole scene seemed absurd and unreal. Stephen's presence among them was eternally bringing up new complications. Could not Negroes and whites ever get together and act like normal individuals or must there always be this awareness of color and this striving to gain favor?

He had noticed the languishing looks which Janet had bestowed upon Stephen, but he knew what close friends she and Aline were, and he had taken for granted that neither were serious enough about Stephen to precipitate jealousy. And Stephen had certainly shown which one he preferred. Of all the damn...

Janet had mentioned Barbara. And he had answered: "We're just good friends." Good friends? He considered their experiences together.

Barbara, Countess Barbara Nitsky. That was the name which had been mumbled to him months ago when they had been introduced at a party. No, it hadn't been at a party. It had been at a dance, at the far famed Alexander Lodge masquerade.

Paul had found Barbara, a pale, slender person with ardent

hazel eyes. She had worn a Florentine costume. Its fragile texture clung to her body and revealed her boyish figure. Her cheeks were pale, her lips a straight red gash, her hair a massive auburn crown studded with brilliants.

"This," Paul had announced with a flourish, "is Countess Nitsky."

She had acknowledged the introduction. Her eyes had sparkled. The lips had parted. She had smiled and remained in their box for the rest of the evening.

It had been impossible to dance, for the floor beneath them was already too packed for anyone else to venture forth. Raymond and Barbara had been drawn together, and had pointed out choice costumes or amusing incidents one to the other. They had had a most enjoyable time, and from then on had often been in one another's company.

Raymond thought of all this now. Thought of the gay comradeship which had developed between them. And wondered, momentarily, if he too was similar to the other Negroes he knew, who deemed it such an honor to possess a white woman. No. He was not like that. White people to him were no novelty. Nor was friendship with them any strange event in his life. He had been reared among them, and had had, thanks to the environment in which he had been born, as much traffic with whites as he had had with Negroes. He could no more deify one of them than he could deify a Negro. They were all creatures of the earth, some of whom he liked, and others for whom he cared nothing whatsoever.

But then. . . he remembered a conversation he had had with Barbara. It had followed his asking her if she was really a countess, after Samuel had assured him that she was nothing of the kind, that she was, to the contrary, a Jewish girl who had been born in the Bronx, sophisticated in Greenwich Village, where she had fallen in love and been deserted by an erudite dilettante from Chicago, and had then migrated to Harlem, broke and discouraged, to dis cover that among Negro men she could be enthroned. and honored like a queen of the realm.

She had been surprisingly frank with Raymond.

"The title and everything is a joke, Ray. Someone called me that the first night I attended a Harlem party and didn't want to give my right name. I have been known as the countess ever since."

"That is funny."

"It's funnier than you think. I heard you arguing with Samuel about Negroes the other day, and it reminded me of a number of things. Have you seen the *Harlem News* this week?"

"Yes."

"Did you notice how my name was flung all over the society page?"

"I never read that junk."

"Well. . . the countess was here and the countess was there. It's beginning to get awful."

"Don't you enjoy it?"

"I'm not entirely a rat, Ray. I do have some feeling. . . even though I couldn't very well give up a profitable living."

"I don't get the connection."

"Well, I have to live. I'm washed up downtown, the more so since I've come to Harlem. And I can get better treatment and more money from colored men than I could ever make downtown with my limited looks and lack of any special ability to put me in the limelight. When I first came up here, I enjoyed it. Everybody made such a fuss over me. But now it makes me sad."

"Why?"

"I see through it all. It's tragic to realize that your Negro men are all so eager to possess a white woman, no matter what her antecedents or present condition. And I'm not talking about the lowbrows, men like Bull, for instance, who just take you casually as they would any woman, then bid you goodbye, even though they may brag for months afterwards. No, I'm talking about your professional men. . . your doctors, lawyers, dentists, business men, and social service workers, especially the latter. They do so much yawping about racial injustice and for racial solidarity, and then when someone like me comes along and gives them the glad eye, they fall over one another in the rush. It's tragic."

"Much more disgusting than tragic, Barbara. But why the hell should you care? If you don't string them along, someone else will. If they want to dine, wine and tip you silver, let 'em. I hope you bleed them well, then write your reminiscences."

Barbara's revelations were not new to Raymond. He had observed similar antics ever since his arrival in Harlem, and had laughed about them. But when women he knew intimately began to fight over his best friend, merely because he was a white man well. . . as Stephen had said, there seemed to be no end to the complexes Negroes had managed to store within themselves.

He was still sitting as Janet had left him, the book review temporarily forgotten, when Stephen sauntered into the room.

"Jesus Christ, I'm tired. I've been in that damn library for hours. Just about one more thesis, and I'll. . . "

"I'm glad you came in, Steve."

"You don't look very joyful." He threw his books down on the table. "Did you finish your review?"

"Yeah. . . with difficulties."

"What kind of difficulties?"

"Yours, Steve."

"Mine?. . . Say. . . what the hell's eating you tonight?"

"Your love affairs."

"Will you talk sense? Or are you drunk?"

"Janet's been talking to me about you."

"What've I done to her?"

"She says she loves you."

"Horse collar."

"She says you prefer Aline to her, because Aline's almost white, but she's going to make you despite her brown skin."

"Are you completely nuts?"

"I'm not that imaginative, Steve."

"But I've hardly noticed the girl, since I've been chasing

with Aline."

"Since? Then you have given her a play?"

"Oh, hell, I've kissed her, I guess, when I was drunk, and she's asked me to take her out every night for the past week but I've always had a date with Aline, and couldn't. I didn't think she was serious."

"Well, she thinks she is. She's all het up to have a white man. Since you're the most desirable one in sight you'd better give her a break."

"I'm not that ambitious."

"Must you be monogamous? Go ahead, give the girl something to be thrilled about."

"Ray. . . you're the damndest. . . what's eating you anyhow? If I thought–"

He was interrupted by Paul bursting excitedly into the room.

"What the hell do you want?" Raymond asked angrily.

"Come on downstairs, both of you."

"For what?"

"We're gonna pray for gin, and we need reinforcements."

"Grand idea, Paul. Come on, Ray. I feel both thirsty and pious, and I'm sure you need gin."

"Oh all right, but I wish to hell you people would leave me alone some time."

There was the usual crowd. Aline, Bull, Pelham, Eustace, and Janet who stared fixedly at Stephen as he entered the room. They were all sitting in a circle holding hands. Three empty chairs awaited the arrival of Stephen, Raymond and Paul. Silently, they took their places. Eustace was master of ceremonies.

"Beloved, we join hands here to pray for gin. An aridity defiles us. Our innards thirst for the juice of juniper. Something must be done. The drought threatens to destroy us. Surely, God who let manna fall from the heavens so that the holy children of Israel might eat, will not let the equally holy children of Niggeratti Manor die from the want of a little gin. Children, let us pray."

All heads were bowed, according to a familiar ritual. Reverently, Eustace patted his foot and rolled his head heavenward.

"Oh, Lord," he began. The others joined in. "Lord, send us some gin. Oh, Lord, send us someone with some money to buy gin, or visit thyself upon the bartender on the corner and make him allow us credit. Father in heaven, we bend before thee. Hear, oh hear, our plea. Send us some gin, Lord, send us some gin."

The prayer finished, the circle remained intact with bowed heads and joined hands. A low moan escaped, a moan such as is often heard in darky camp meetings. It grew in volume and swelled melodiously throughout the room. Abruptly it stopped. Eustace had spoken:

"And, Lord, send me a little sandwich too."

X

The prayer was not answered immediately, and in time everyone became gloomy and morose. Since no one came in with money to buy gin, it was thought expedient for Raymond to go to the corner speakeasy and attempt to chisel two bottles from the bartender, promising payment at a later date. But this Raymond refused to do. He, himself, was not over-anxious for a drink, and consequently felt no interest in whether the others had any or not.

He kept a close watch on Aline, Janet and Stephen, expecting an outburst, but Janet contented herself, sitting apart from the rest, glowering at Aline, who retaliated by snuggling closer into Stephen's arms as if to advertise her priority. Paul attempted to enliven the group with one of his fantastic tales, but by now everyone was familiar with almost any tale Paul could tell, and paid so little attention to what he said that he soon gave up, and sauntered out of the room, saying that he was going for a walk.

Bull alone seemed to be in good humor, and finally announced that since no one else would move a finger, he would sally forth and return with enough gin to "ossify the whole damn bunch o' you."

Eustace cornered Raymond, and began his usual lament about his lack of opportunity. It annoyed him considerably that so many young and unknown Negro singers were getting hearings from Broadway audiences, while he, older, more experienced, and more musically learned, must be content with infrequent and disappointing Harlem appearances. He wanted to branch out and entrance larger and more discriminating audiences than Harlem offered, but every attempt he had made to get in a Broadway show, or arrange for a radio or concert audition, had ended in failure. Raymond knew why this was, but he knew there was no use sharing this knowledge with Eustace.

He was tired, though, of continually listening to Eustace's

wails, and made up his mind then and there to consul: Samuel about the matter, and see what that energetic soul could do.

Bull did not return. There seemed to be no hope for getting any gin. The prayers of the holy children of Niggeratti Manor had met with no results. Raymond eased himself away from Eustace and returned to his studio and to his book review. Pelham, too, had deserted the would-be revelers, and secluded himself in his room where he set about put ting on the finishing touches to a portrait he had just finished, a portrait of Pavlowa, copied out of the *New York Times* Rotogravure supplement. Only Aline, Janet, Stephen and Eustace remained downstairs. Eustace was finding solace in the piano and in song. He had opened a portfolio of songs by Shubert and was running through the entire group. Janet still sat in her corner, glowering at the interlocked couple on the bed. Finally she spoke.

"I'm going home."

"Don't let me stop you," Aline answered. "The key's in my pocketbook."

"I don't need your keys. I'm not living at your house anymore." With which she stalked out of the room.

Stephen would have followed, but Aline re strained him.

"Never mind, baby. She has nowhere else to go. She'll be right there in the bed where she belongs when I get home."

Nothing else happened. Eustace continued to sing. Aline and Stephen, tired of spooning in such a depressive atmosphere, decided to go to a motion picture show. The night was singularly dull and uneventful.

Early the next morning, Raymond telephoned Samuel and asked him to come up as soon as possible. Always willing to be of service, and always eager to know just what was going on in Niggeratti Manor, Samuel dropped everything and immediately made his way to Harlem.

"What is it Ray?" he asked before removing his hat and coat.

"Nothing exciting, Sam. I just want you to see what you can do to help Eustace get an audition downtown. Make him some contacts. Of course he can't sing, but give him a break. I've heard worse, and," he added slyly, "you're always bemoaning the fact that none of us will let you champion our cause. Here's your chance to make an impression."

Samuel set to work immediately. He interviewed many people who were figures in the concert world, and finally located a group who not only promised to grant Eustace an audition, but who also said that if his voice was all Samuel claimed, they, themselves, would present him in a concert of songs at Carnegie Hall.

Exultingly, Samuel rushed back uptown to tell Eustace the good news. Raymond entered the room soon after his arrival, and was startled to find Eustace angrily pacing the room. He had been apprised by telephone of what Samuel had done, and had expected to find Eustace most joyful. It did not take him long to discover what was wrong.

"But I won't sing spirituals," Eustace declared.

"Why won't you sing them?" Samuel asked. "They're your heritage. You shouldn't be ashamed of them."

"What makes you think they're my heritage, Sam? I have no relationship with the people who originated them. Furthermore I'm a musician, and as far as I can see, spirituals are most certainly not music."

"Nonsense."

"It's not nonsense. Aren't there enough people already spurting those bastard bits of doggerel? Must every Negro singer dedicate his life to the crooning of slave songs?"

"But they're beautiful," Raymond interjected.

"Beautiful?" There was scorn in his voice.

"Beautiful because they are now the fad. I'm a concert singer, and I won't be untrue to my art."

"Roland Hayes sings them," Samuel announced as if this should put an end to all objections.

"Yes, as a sop. He throws them to his audience because they want them, because they are unwilling to listen to a Negro sing an entire program of classical music. I'm no slave and I won't sing slave music if I never have a concert."

He sat down abruptly at the piano and began striking haphazard chords. Samuel appealed to Raymond.

"Isn't there anything you can say? These people are most willing to help him. Can't you make him understand that he must make some compromise?"

Raymond shrugged his shoulders. He had done his bit, and he now had little interest in the matter. He was conversant with Eustace's objections to singing spirituals, and to him, these objections were silly, unintelligent, and indefensible. He had no sympathy whatsoever with Negroes like Eustace, who contended that should their art be Negroid, they, the artist, must be considered inferior. As if a poem or a song or a novel by and about Negroes could not reach the same heights as a poem or a song or a novel by or about any other race. Eustace did not realize that by adhering to such a belief, he also subscribed to the theory of Nordic superiority. Yet there was nothing to be done about it. Eustace by refusing to sing spirituals was only hurting himself. And the world would miss nothing if he should die unheard. He had the urge to sing, and he also had a good church choir voice, but on the concert stage he could be at best only one of the mediocre also rans.

Samuel was irate.

"I think you're a damn fool."

"All artists are considered damn fools by Philistines," was the withering retort.

"This argument gets you nowhere," Raymond said. "Both of you are being childish."

"Who wouldn't be childish?" Samuel shouted. "These people have promised to give Eustace an audition. I tooted his horn good and plenty. It may mean the making of him. What I can't make him understand is that he can sing all the Schubert, Schumann, Handel, Brahms, Beethoven or anything else he wishes, but he must expect a request for spirituals. And if he isn't prepared, the whole thing will be called off."

"I have no further interest in the matter. I will not sing

spirituals."

And having thus firmly declared himself, he resumed his striking of harmonic chords. These darky folk songs had become his *bête noir*. On several different occasions now, he had been asked to sing before informal gatherings, and each time the crowd had snickered when he had loftily refused to sing spirituals. Moreover, the snickers had continued throughout his repertoire of Schubert, Mozart, Friml, Herbert and Strauss. And even his spirited denunciation of Dvorak's inclusion of a Negro folk song in the *New World Symphony* had provoked not only argument but ridicule. The white people now entering the social world of Negroes were bringing about disturbing changes. Eustace wished to leave these old mammy songs alone; he also wanted to sing in an auspicious downtown auditorium, but it seemed as if no one would back him unless spirituals were listed on the program.

He must, it seemed, capitulate, although in his opinion there was a sufficient number of darkies already shaming contemporary Negroes by singing these barbarous, moaning shouts and too simple melodies. If Robeson, Taylor Gordon, Rosemond Johnson, Roland Hayes, Service Bell, the Hall Johnson Choirs, and many others were all acquiescing to this new demand, why should he not be different and remain the singer of classics he innately was?

Raymond motioned to Samuel. They left the room together and went to Raymond's studio.

"What am I to do, Ray?"

"Leave him alone for a few days. Meanwhile I'll post everyone in the house to keep harping on his good luck in finally finding downtown backing. He'll give in. He's just about at his rope's end now."

"But why should he be so stubborn?"

"Because he was probably brought up to despise anything which reminded his elders of slavery."

"I have no patience with him."

"You should have. That's part of your calling. It is funny, though and exasperating. I can just picture his family. They're

New Englanders, like you. There was probably a grandfather who had been a slave. Perhaps he was a free Negro and had mi grated north. He probably raised his children to despise anything reminiscent of his days of servitude. Dialect stories were an abomination. Spirituals only to be regarded as unfortunate echoes from the auction block and the whipping post. Came Eustace on the scene. He was destined to become a singer after his primary voice experiments as an adolescent. They probably found him some high-toned white teacher with musty ideas. This teacher probably filled young Eustace's musical craw with pseudo-classical ideals, ideals essentially saccharine and sentimental. Which accounts for what we now have on our hands."

"But he has the audacity to want to sing opera."

"And you know as well as I that he could hardly make it on the concert stage. Negroes, though, have rated him high, higher than Hayes or Robe son. Why? He strives to be a carbon copy of Caruso. He sings at a church or lodge benefit. What does he sing? The aria from Pagliacci. And as an encore renders all the other flashy bits from turgid operas he can learn. You better leave Eustace to me, Sam. You lack tact. I bet you three dinners, I'll have him downtown in time for that audition."

"The bet's on, Ray, but I think you're cuckoo."

XI

Niggeratti Manor was in a ferment.

It seemed as if everyone in the house on this particular day was unusually active. From the basement came the lugubrious wailings of Eustace as he finally began the serious practice of spirituals. His conversion had been slow. It had necessitated much cajoling, flattery and diplomatic argument, but he had finally been won over. His piano was now cleared of his beloved classic music which he had tenderly wrapped in luxurious packets of green velvet and laid away in a cedar chest. The time for his audition was approaching rapidly.

Eloquently had he announced his plans to Raymond.

"Yes, I'll sing spirituals. And I'll also astound them with the rest of my repertoire. I'll make them appreciate my talent. And I'll sing the classics so much better than spirituals that they'll realize which is my metier."

Then with a grimace of distaste he had set about learning *Ezekiel Saw the Wheel.*

Raymond was busy writing a magazine article. He had locked his door and dared anyone to interrupt him. Paul remained downstairs with Eustace, amusing himself by conceiving a series of designs to illustrate Carl Van Vechten's *Nigger Heaven.* Stephen was away from home, working at the library, collecting data for his doctor's thesis.

Pelham meanwhile was putting the finishing touches on his *magnum opus,* a portrait of two girls, daughters of the lady who lived in the rear room on the third floor. This lady professed to be an actress, but so far her appearances had been confined to Harlem church socials and lodge benefits. She took her histrionic career quite seriously, so seriously in fact that she refused to do any other type of work and somehow managed to support herself and her two daughters on the small weekly pittance she received from her estranged husband.

No one in the house, except Pelham, ever had much traffic

with the lady, outside of the conventional greeting should they happen to meet either her or her offspring on the stairs. She had made overtures of friendship and had even crashed certain of their parties, but they had always treated her like a complete outsider. She made no appeal to any of them either as a person or as an artist. Consequently they ignored her.

Pelham was different. He was always giving her a portion of the cakes or pies he constantly made. He would also cut out paper animals and color them for the adolescent girls. Hardly a day passed that they did not invade his room to watch him work. It was inevitable that he should finally suggest painting their portraits, for Pelham was eternally in search of new models, and having used Raymond, Stephen, Eustace and Paul again and again, he was eager for fresh subjects.

There also lived on the third floor a mysterious, witch-like person, labeled the Pig Woman by Raymond, because of her resemblance to an outstanding character in a contemporary *cause celebre*. She was aged, wrinkled and black. Her torso was the shape of an arc, and she limped as she walked along mumbling to herself. It was not known how long she had been living in the house. Euphoria had found her there. She still remained. Three times per week the left home at six in the morning and she always returned exactly twelve hours later. The other days she remained at home, unheard, unseen—a silent mysterious person who held converse with no one in the house except herself. Nor was she ever known to have visitors.

Raymond remembered vividly his first glimpse of her. He had just moved into the house. He, Paul, Eustace and Pelham were arranging the furniture in his room and hanging pictures on the wall. Suddenly their ears had been ravaged by a series of hoarse, guttural shrieks as if coming from the throat of a wounded parrot. Frightened, they had rushed into the hall, where they had seen the Pig Woman leaning over the banisters wildly gesticulating. They had run up the stairs, eager to know the cause of the disturbance. With palsied fingers she had pointed to a stray bat blindly beating itself against the ceiling. Pelham had run for a broom. Eustace had leaned back against the wall, gathering the folds of his green dressing gown tightly about him. Raymond had tried to silence the old lady. Paul had stood by and laughed.

In a few moments Pelham had returned with the broom and after a wild scurry succeeded in knocking the blind intruder to the floor. Paul had wrapped it tightly in newspaper and, taking the parcel to the cellar, burned it in the furnace.

The Pig Woman had been distraught.

"Evil spirits, I tell you. Evil spirits. Dat's bad luck. Dis house is doomed. De people in it are damned."

And she had stumbled into her room eerily sobbing to herself.

Before nightfall of this singularly hard-working day, Pelham had completed his masterpiece. So elated was he over what he declared to be a remarkable resemblance to his subjects, and a crafty blending of colors, that he bounced around the house like a rubber ball, exhibiting his canvas to all within. The picture was atrocious, but no one was heartless enough to disillusion him. No one told him that there was not even the slightest resemblance between portrait and subject. No one winced openly at the blurred features, or at the hideously colored and highly incongruous background. Neither did anyone, save the girls and their mother, praise his handiwork. Being used to the reticence of the others, he accepted it as suppressed appreciation.

His joy was complete when the mother of the girls asked him to give her the picture and also to pen her an accompanying poem. Anxious to make the poem a fitting complement to the portraits, he announced that he would be unable to prepare dinner that night. The muse must function this one time uninterrupted by menial duties. He then shut himself up in his studio, and the eavesdropper could hear the scratch of his pen and the occasional crumpling of unsatisfactory sheets of paper.

It fell to Paul to cook the dinner. Raymond had not expected him to volunteer, but he had, and had asked only that he be left alone. He was to prepare meat balls and spaghetti and a lettuce and tomato salad. This he did in a surprisingly short time, and his announcement of the meal was eloquent.

Three times Eustace went for Pelham before he could be persuaded to come to dinner, and, when he did arrive, he brought his manuscript to the table, ignoring the food placed before him while he continued to work. Even the uproar occasioned by Stephen's asking why the spaghetti was sweet and Paul's admitting that he had poured the contents of the sugar bowl into the kettle, failed to divert Pelham from his chosen creative task. The poem must be finished and it must be good. The lady had promised to present both the poem and the portrait of her daughters to her art club, and she was certain that many of her friends would commission him to do their portraits, and that the club would request him to design and write verses for Christmas cards, programs and reception favors. The cognoscenti might scoff or remain enviously silent. The public would acclaim, and he would at last reap the fruit of his sowing.

George Jones, for that was Pelham's real name, did not remember either his father or his mother. He remembered only a woman he called grandmother and with whom he had migrated from Virginia to New Jersey with a family of white people while still an infant. This grandmother had been a servant in the house since her birth in slavery. Her parents before her had served the same family. They were the type of Negro who had refused freedom and who had remained with "ole miss" and "ole master" until their death. Grandmother Mack had lived, too, only to serve the children of her parents' master. And when one of the younger girls had married and moved north, Grandmother Mack had come, too, determined to see that her mistress' daughter did not suffer for want of care.

George was not her grandson, nor was he any relation to her whatsoever. He was a stray pickaninny whom no one claimed and for whom she had developed an affection because, as she phrased it, "he was so consarned black." No one objected to her adopting the apparently parentless pickaninny, nor had her white folks objected when she brought him north with her.

In his youth, George knew nothing but the kitchen, the backyard, the basement and the alley way. He ran errands for his white folk and for Grandma Mack. He also assisted the old lady in the kitchen and in the laundry room, and, as he grew older, he was promoted to waiting upon the table. making up the beds, washing the windows, sweeping the floors, dusting the furniture, and ironing the flat work.

He went to school only because his white folk insisted upon it. Grandma Mack had no patience with those hifalutin' niggers who tried to emulate white folks. Niggers were made to be servants. God had willed it. And only through a life of servitude could they hope to obtain an entry into heaven. They were the sons of Ham who had been cursed for looking upon his father's nakedness. They were also the children of Cain who had been cursed and made black for murdering his brother, Abel. Schools were for white folk. These modern niggers made Grandma Mack angry, always talking about education, prating about social equality, criticizing the superior pale face. If they remained in their places, accepted the menial positions to which they were entitled instead of trying to usurp the parlor, they would not have to worry about being lynched, jim-crowed and otherwise put in their place. Grandma Mack had never forgiven Abraham Lincoln for freeing the slaves. Nor could she forgive him for sending hordes of uncouth Yankees into the Southland to rape, pillory and otherwise molest the only truly genteel folk in the United States. Venomously did she regard northern whites, and savagely did she denounce northern blacks.

In this atmosphere had George continued his en forced schooling. His homework always remained undone, because his home duties were so numerous. Grandma Mack was older now, almost too old and infirm of limb to do much else besides cook and supervise George. It was amazing the amount of work her diminutive black charge managed to do.

When George was fourteen an older son of the house had been sent to Europe. He was going to be an artist, a portrait painter. After a year abroad he had returned home, laden down with lithographic reproductions of the old masters, and almost daily he received copies of art magazines from continental capitals. These latter items eventually became George's property. He mulled over them constantly, and was stirred by the brilliant colors and voluptuous figures which decorated some of the pages. George also took great pride in cleaning up his young master's attic studio. He would linger there under pretense of being busy, finger the brushes, the paint pots, the canvases, and, when he was certain of not being interrupted, would often posture in front of a mirror with a palette.

He was going to be an artist. Taking toilet paper he would place it over the pictures in the various magazines and use it for tracing paper, later transferring the copied reproduction on to smoothed out sheets of wrapping paper or maltreated paper bags.

He was going to be an artist. His schoolbooks were defaced with malodorous pictures of his fellow students, all of whom, according to their delineator, were possessed of well-rounded bodies, prominent nostrils, slit eyes, and perpendicular ears. At home he formed fantastic designs in his soapy dish water. When he washed windows he used Bon Ami so that he might trace figures on the surface of the glass as he rubbed it clean. And the peeling of potatoes or apples was a constant exercise in fancy carving.

When he was twenty years of age, Grandma Mack had died. Her white folks had her savings account transferred to one for George. They also deposited to this account the small sum she had coming from a Metropolitan Life Insurance policy which they had taken out for her. George obtained his bank book by stealth, withdrew the money, and boarded a ferry boat bound for New York. He had decided to risk all in order to gain fame and fortune as an artist.

Native intuition saved him from immediate disaster. Promptly upon arriving, he sought a job, and obtained one as valet to an actor. In this position he was most happy, being able congenially to combine his two professions. He lived in his employer's apartment, attended to all his wants, and continued the painting of pictures and the writing of verse in his spare time. All was well until he happened across Euphoria Blake's advertisement in the *Harlem News* announcing "congenial studios for Negro artists." That was what he wanted. He telephoned Euphoria immediately, reserved a studio, stocked up with paints, charcoal, modeling clay, brushes, scalpels, palettes, easels, watercolors, and everything else the clerk in the art store suggested he might need, changed his name to Pelham Gaylord, and dedicated his life to the serious business of being an artist.

He was overjoyed when Raymond moved into the house. For it had been bruited about that he was soon to emerge as one of the black hopes of Negro literature. George also knew that most of Raymond's friends were in some measure known to the public for their poems, stories or drawings. Their names were often mentioned in magazine and newspaper articles. This was just the group he needed to know, just the people he should cultivate. To be in such company was Pelham's conception of heaven. He considered them as gods far up the Mount Olympus he himself was trying to scale. After knowing them, he was frankly ill at ease in their company, quite often shocked by their conversation, and obviously disturbed by the presence of their white friends whom they accepted so casually. Nevertheless he was determined to learn, determined to observe and assimilate. He must be like them.

It came to be a matter of routine that he should clean their studios, prepare the communal meals, wash the dishes, and act as a servant when they had company. Raymond, Eustace and Paul accepted this service, politely encouraged him in his art, and kept a straight face when without warning he would burst in upon them, black face wreathed in smiles, proudly to exhibit a new picture or a new poem. Dutifully did they sit for him to do their portraits.

The extent of his ineptitude was abysmal. Quietly they suggested that he attend an art school, then immediately knew they had said the wrong thing, for Pelham had native talent, which he himself was going to develop. Artists were not made in schools. A phrase of their own was flung at them triumphantly. Paul told him he was a Dadaist. Eustace, Raymond and Euphoria acquiesced. Only Stephen scoffed, and his scoffing was discounted by Pelham, because Stephen was white, and white people would naturally resent a black genius.

By the time all had finished eating, Pelham had finally finished his poem. Triumphantly he threw his fountain pen into his plate of untouched food, and waved his piece of paper before them. No one encouraged him to read what he had written and he remained impervious to the covert conversation of mischievous eyes. He accepted their silence as a request for an immediate rendition. Gleefully, he read:

> *"I paint on canvas And on paper*
> *Charms of girlhood All a-flutter*
> *Youthful bloom, Beauteous maidens*
> *On life's threshold.*
>
> *"You who charm the artist's brush*
> *You who guide his fountain pen*
> *You who bring the spirit solace*
> *With your trusting innocence.*
>
> *"Beauteous maidens, gracious mother,*
> *E'en the sun don't always shine.*
> *Life is real, and fate is earnest.*
> *God will guide you to his shrine*
> *Of eternal happiness."*

He finished and beamed at his audience. They sheepishly avoided his gaze and earnestly tried to think of something appropriate to say. No one laughed. No one even felt the urge to snicker. It was impossible to ridicule when his voice was so tender, his eyes so bright, his smile so pleased and ingratiating. There was complete silence. The eyes no longer conversed. Pelham's black face shone with satisfaction. His audience had been stirred, moved, affected by the pathos and beauty of his poem. But he was not concerned with them. He must rush to those for whom it was intended. Still beaming, he pushed his chair back from the table, and hastened from the kitchen. They could hear him noisily running up the stairs.

Everyone was saddened. Even Paul was pensive. Conversation was desultory and lagged. Stephen was surly. Eustace hurried to his studio and could soon be heard softly singing *Water Boy*. Raymond struck a match to light a cigarette, and burned his lip before he realized that the cigarette was still lying on the table, where he had placed it while he found the matches. But even this performance elicited no comment, realized no audience. Stephen muttered something about the damn dishes and went out of the room. A moment later the front door slammed. Paul and Raymond stacked the dishes in the sink, con versing meanwhile in subdued tones about the multiplying cockroaches. Their task finished they both went out into the street. Paul to roam the avenue. Raymond to meet Lucille. And on the top floor, in the little coffin shaped studio, Pelham read and reread his poem to an appreciative audience.

XII

When Raymond arrived at the subway kiosk where they had planned to meet. Lucille was already there. She rushed forward to meet him, a trim tailored figure with a mischievous gleam in her sparkling eyes.

"Gee, Ray. I haven't seen you in a coon's age."

"Your fault, my dear."

"Not so sure. Where do we go. . . to your house?"

"Not yet. Let's have a drink."

After a short walk, they were soon seated in the rear room of their favorite speakeasy, which stood on the corner, one half block removed from Niggeratti Manor. They ordered gin rickies. Lucille noted Ray's depression.

"What are you in the dumps about?"

"Nothing, I suppose, yet everything. I guess that damn house is getting on my nerves."

"Too much whoopee?"

"No, not particularly. Too much everything, and particularly too much Pelham. I can't laugh at him anymore and it hurts."

"Why don't you be frank with him?" Then as Raymond sipped his drink she answered her own question. "No. . . you couldn't be. He wouldn't believe you anyhow."

"People like him should be exterminated."

"He's happier than you."

"I wonder. That's what Tony says. . . to be dumb is to be happy, but to be that dumb!!!!!"

They both laughed.

"That's probably not the kind of dumbness Tony meant; after all there is a difference between being dumb and being stupid."

"Right you are and there is also a difference in being. Oh, hell! Let's forget it." Raymond drained his glass and rang for the bar tender.

"Let's have another."

"Sure."

The bartender acknowledged their signal.

"What have you been doing, 'Cile?"

"Falling in love."

She giggled as she said it.

"Good God," Raymond shouted. "If another woman tells me that, I'm gonna commit murder."

Lucille remained silent as she drained her glass.

"And who, if I may ask, is your beloved?"

"Bull."

"Bull!!"

"Yes, Bull."

"Well, I'll be damned."

"I knew you'd be surprised."

He stared at her unbelievingly, assured that she was joking. He hunted for a gleam of mischief in her eye. There was none.

"When did this begin?"

"Well, I met him at your house a couple of times. He took me home one night when you couldn't be pried away from Barbara."

"Is this retaliation?"

"Not at all. Why should it be?"

"So that's why Bull's been so irrepressible lately."

"Me too."

"But Bull," he advanced weakly, then rang for another rickey. "It's preposterous." For the first time he laughed. "Come on, let's drink." They gulped down their rickies. The bartender was summoned again.

"Now, quit kidding."

"I mean it, Ray. I'm mad about him."

"As Stephen would say, 'Horse Collar.' "

"I admit it's surprising, but after all I have to have my fling sometime or other. I always knew I'd fall for a man of that type."

"Attraction of opposites, I suppose."

"Maybe so, and maybe not, but Bull does represent something I have needed in my life. Damn it all, Ray, there's something in me which revolts against the even, stodgy, prim life I have to lead. I'm sick of being constantly surrounded by sterile white people, and of having to associate with Negroes who are also sterile and pseudo-white. I suppose I find the same thing in Bull that white women claim to find in a man like Jack Johnson. That's the price I pay, evidently, for becoming civilized."

"I think you're as full of hooey as a backyard telephone booth. Jesus, does one ever know one's friends? Must we be treated to these constant surprises? There's Janet gettin' hysterical 'cause she can't have a crack at Stephen an' 'cause her chum beat her to the first white man she ever wanted. An' here's you falling for an ignorant braggart 'cause he's virile. Are you the girl who told me sex meant little to you? Are you still frigid?"

The bartender brought them another pair of rickies. It was his treat.

"Don't be nasty, Ray."

"Maybe I'm jealous."

"Nonsense."

"Why is it nonsense? I ain't human, I guess."

"Sure, you're human, plenty much. And maybe you're jealous, but not from the accepted causes."

"Oh, no-oo?"

"No. You're too much in love with yourself ever to love anyone. You're jealous only because so much has happened without your knowledge. Had I made you believe you engineered the thing you'd be happy."

"Didn't you tell me not to be nasty?" Raymond forced a smile. Lucille had touched a vulnerable spot. "Nevertheless, you can't blame me for being upset. Prim Yankee maiden falls for Harlem bruiser. Educated girl gives self to burly rousta-bout."

He began to laugh. "Jesus, this is good." Lucille was still self-possessed.

"Bull may be ignorant, a roustabout, and a bruiser, but at least he's a man, and knows how to get what he wants."

The bartender stood over their table. Lucille ordered

another pair of rickies. There was an incisive, angry gleam in Raymond's eyes.

"What do you mean by that?" he asked when they were alone again.

"Forget it. Let's go to the house."

"I ain't goin' nowhere till you 'splain."

"An' I ain't gonna 'splain."

"Dammit all, 'Cile. . . " The bartender returned before he could finish. Lucille handed him a five dol lar bill, then swiftly downing her drink, got up from the table and crossed the room to a mirror, adjusted her hat, powdered her face, received her change, and started from the room. Raymond staggered slightly as he rose to follow her.

A few minutes later they stumbled noisily into Raymond's studio. Paul was there, indolently coloring a series of voluptuous geometric designs which he characterized as spirit portraits. Stephen and Aline were curled up on a corner of the daybed, heads together, intimately whispering. Barbara was on the floor beside Paul, watching and admiring his deft and easy brush manipulations. Samuel was sitting as usual, bolt upright in one of the wicker chairs, solemn of countenance, frowning at the couple on the bed. Eustace and Janet were sharing the other wicker chair, reading from *Fine Clothes to the Jew*, Langston Hughes' latest book of poems. Behind their chair was Bull, his bulky shadow darkening the book's pages. Pelham was in the kitchenette, mixing drinks.

"Hi, everybody," Lucille and Raymond shouted in unison. "We're high as kites."

Bull frowned as Lucille swayed toward him. He took her in his arms and guided her way to the couch. They sat down in the corner opposite from the one occupied by Aline and Stephen. Raymond watched them jealously.

"Why in the hell don't someone make some noise? Start the victrola, Samuel."

"Pipe down, son," Bull growled. Lucille's head slumped to his shoulder.

"I want music, I tell you," Raymond continued shrilly. "I

must have music. The world's crazy. I want jazz, crazy as the world."

He stood in the center of the room, disheveled, gesticulating, shouting:

> "Drink gin, drink gin.
> Drink gin with me goddam.
> I don't give a damn
> Who won't drink gin with me, goddam.
> For no damn man
> Go to hell. Sonofabitch—Oh—"

Barbara got up from the floor and started toward him. He pushed her away, staggered into the alcove, gulped down one of the drinks Pelham had prepared, then lurched back into the room and flopped himself down beside Paul. Barbara joined him. Pelham passed the drinks. Raymond giggled:

"Paul's gone phallic again. Hey, Sam, seen this?"

Barbara drew his head into her lap. Paul's brush continued its swift strokes. Lucille had gone to sleep on Bull's shoulder. The others drained their glasses.

"Read out loud, Eustace," Barbara commanded. Eustace arched his eyebrows and in his best theatrical manner intoned Langston Hughes' poem:

> *"I am your son, white man!*
> *Georgia dusk*
> *And the turpentine woods,*
> *One of the pillars of the temple fell.*
> *You are my son!*
> *Like hell!*

> *"The moon over the turpentine woods*
> *The southern night*
> *Full of stars*
> *Great big yellow stars.*

> *"Juicy bodies*
> *Of nigger wenches*

Blue black
Against black fences.
O, you little bastard boy
What's a body but a toy?

"The scent of pine wood in the evening air

"A nigger night,
A nigger joy,
A little yellow
Bastard boy."

"Marvelous," Barbara exclaimed.

"Disgusting," Samuel shot through compressed lips.

Raymond was aroused. "How d'y' figure disgusting?"

"It's an insult to any self-respecting Negro."

"How come?" Raymond's head abruptly left Barbara's lap. He sat on his haunches as if ready to spring, glaring directly into Samuel's face. "How come, I say?"

"It's vulgar. Moreover why should one of your poets prate publicly about your yellow bastard boys? You ought to be ashamed of them."

"How come?" Raymond reiterated defiantly.

"Shut up, both of you." Stephen knew that Raymond was drunk. "Fix us another drink, Pelham."

"Ain't gonna shut up. Gonna make Samuel tell me what he means. I'm sick of his *ex 'thedra* 'nouncements 'bout the race. I don't think he knows a damn thing 'bout it."

"All right, we agree," Stephen interpolated.

Raymond continued stubbornly. "Yeah. He's a misfit white tryin' to become a latter day ab'lish ionist. He's makin' a career of Negroes. He comes here to direct and patronize. He knows so much more 'bout what we ought to do an' feel cause he's white an' he's read soshology."

"Hush, sweet," Barbara pleaded and placed her hands on his shoulders.

"Ain't gonna hush. Gonna tell him what I think. Gonna

say what I think 'bout all these meddlin' whites. They oughta stay outa Harlem."

"Are you becoming a race purist?" Stephen sought to draw Raymond's attention to him.

"Hell, no. But that's what Samuel thinks I oughta be. He frowns at you an' Aline. He scowls at me an' Barbara. He tells me privately Barbara ain't nothin' but a common hussy. Then he gets her an' lectures 'bout her losin' self-respect bein' intimate with Negroes."

Samuel flushed more deeply than before.

"You're drunk and damn insulting."

"I ain't drunk. An' I'm jes tellin' you the truth. You can't stand to see a Negro and a white woman friends, can you? You believe in social equality. Oh, yes. You'd even marry a colored girl if one'd have a nincompoop like you. But white women are sacred. You're a pukin' hypocrite. If you can't stand the gaff you oughta get out for good."

Samuel leaped to his feet. His face was brick red. His eyes cold and angry. His lips quivered.

"That's what I say about you Negroes. You don't know a friend when you have one. You don't know how to treat decent white people who mean you good. You'd rather lick the boots of trash."

"You want me to lick your boots, don't you? You goddamned sonofabitch." Raymond dashed the contents of his half empty glass into Samuel's face. Samuel's foot shot into the air and kicked Raymond on the side of his head. The room was in an uproar. Bull pushed Lucille's head from his shoulder and started for Samuel. Stephen attempted to hold him back. Lucille slumped unconscious to the couch. Aline and Janet screamed. Eustace sat perched on the edge of his chair, twiddling the book he held, murmuring: "Mercy, mercy," over and over again. Pelham stood transfixed against the door, a tray of empty glasses in his hand. Paul made a desperate, futile effort to rescue his drawings as Samuel was floored by Bull's fist.

"Kick 'im, will ya?" Bull was raving mad. "You lousy white

trash, I'll stomp your dirty guts out."

Only Stephen's tackle of his legs prevented Bull from carrying out this ghastly threat.

XIII

Y ou made rather an ass out of yourself last night."

"To the contrary, I would say I made asses out of the rest of you." Raymond was irritable and mordant. Stephen sat on the side of the bed examining red bruises on his arms and legs. "I didn't want to fight. I didn't ask the rest of you to fight."

"That's why you threw your liquor in Samuel's face. Just a friendly gesture, eh?"

"He deserved it. Damn it all, my patience with him is fretted out. I was probably woozily illogical last night, but, as I remember, I gave him a much deserved tongue lashing. Don't you realize what a pest he and his type are? Zora Hurston has named them Negrotarians, which when analyzed is most apt. They are as bad as those eloquent, oleaginous Negro crusaders and men of God, who sit in mahogany office chairs or else stand behind pulpits and thunder invective to Negroes against whites. The Negrotarians have a formula, too. They have regimented their sympathies and fawn around Negroes with a cry in their heart and a superiority bug in their head. It's a new way to get a thrill, a new way to merit distinction in the community cultivating Negroes. It's a sure way to bolster up. . . this their own weak ego and cut a figure. Negroes being what they are make this sort of person possible."

"Which means?"

Raymond replied sharply: "That ninety-nine and ninety-nine hundredths percent of the Negro race is patiently possessed and motivated by an inferiority complex. Being a slave race actuated by slave morality, what else could you expect? Within themselves and by their every action they subscribe to the doctrine of Nordic superiority and the louder they cry against it the more they mark themselves inferiors. Of course they are flattered by whites like Samuel, flattered to be verbally accepted as equals by someone who mayhap mentally is their inferior. But as long as he has a white skin it's all right. In the white world what is Samuel? A nonentity who doesn't count. Among Negroes. . . my God, he's a king, looked up to, pursued. And look at Barbara, absolutely down and out until she chanced to come to Harlem. Now every male in the respectable Negro middle class she has invaded longs to possess her. And yourself—"

"What about me?"

"Don't play dumb. You know. You can't help but be aware of the eager subservience they proffer you, both men and women."

"Aren't you generalizing?"

"I said a little while ago. . . ninety-nine and ninety-nine hundredths per cent."

"And that remaining one hundredths per cent?"

"You know as well as I do who it is in this crowd. Lucille, myself, and sometimes Paul. And you also know that we are the only ones around here with whom you can feel natural. The rest force a certain psychological reaction."

"But Bull. . . "

"Is so afraid of the white man," Raymond snapped angrily, "that his only recourse is to floor one at every opportunity and on any pretext. Should one suddenly turn the tables and smash him back he'd run away like a cowed dog."

Stephen laughed. "What's to be done about it?"

"What's to be done about anything? Nothing. Negroes are a slave race and a slave race they'll remain until assimilated. Individuals will arise and escape on the ascending ladder of their own individuality. The others will remain what they are. Their superficial progress means nothing. Instinctively they are still the servile progeny of servile ancestors."

"God, but you love your race this morning. You haven't been so eloquent in weeks."

"Oh, I know they can't help it. I don't condemn. Why should I? They have no free will. . . no choice but to be what their environment and nature. has made them. Fifty per cent of them never think about it. They go about their business, happy in their menial jobs, enjoying themselves while and as they may. The rest. . . .. the educated minority and middle class have that memorable American urge to keep up with the Joneses. Well, let them. But why not face reality and admit what they are? Why invest themselves with possibilities beyond their reach? No intelligent person subscribes to the doc trine of Nordic superiority, but everyone can realize that now the white man has both the power and the money. His star is almost at the zenith of its ascendancy. There are signs of an impending eclipse, but meanwhile he holds the whip. The rest of the races have to dance and imitate. And we all know that this whip is not held by the white masses although the world has been made safe for democracy. The white masses and the black masses must all cater to the masters who hold the money bags. The white masses seemingly have the edge only because of their closer kinship to those in power."

"I don't follow you altogether, Ray. You seem confused. Is this Communism you're preaching?"

"Hell, no. I preach nothing. I don't give a good god damn what becomes of any mass. Communism can no more change their status than democracy, although for the moment we might have the pleasure of seeing our enshrined bourgeoisie lose their valued heads."

"And if that should happen?"

"I'd stand by enjoying the carnage, then pessimistically await the emergence of a similar bunch of dolts to take the places of the deceased."

Stephen finished putting on his clothes.

"You've learned your lessons well."

"What?"

"I say, you've learned your lessons well. Good schoolmasters you've had, too, *n'est-ce pas*?"

He smiled benignly and left the room, before Raymond's confused mind could digest his words or formulate a fitting retort.

XIV

RAYMOND spent most of the afternoon idly wandering about Central Park, stopping at haphazard intervals to rest on a park bench. He had decided that it was time he was taking stock of himself, time he was casting an appraising and critical eye over his past and present, and perhaps in the muddle find a guidepost for the future. He was disturbed and moody. His experiences of the night before and his talk with Stephen this same morning had caused his spirits to become curdled and his mind to become confused. He was going. . . he knew not where. Always he had protested that the average Negro intellectual and artist had no goal, no standards, no elasticity, no pregnant germ plasm. And now he was beginning to doubt even himself.

He wanted to write, but he had made little progress. He wanted to become a Prometheus, to break the chains which held him to a racial rack and carry a blazing beacon to the top of Mount Olympus so that those possessed of Alpine stocks could follow in his wake. He wanted to do something memorable in literature, something that could stay afloat on the contemporary sea of weighted ballast, something which could transcend and survive the transitional age in which he was living. He wanted to accomplish these things, but he was becoming less and less confident that he was possessed of the necessary genius. He did not doubt that he had a modicum of talent, but talent was not a sufficient springboard to guarantee his being catapulted into the literary halls of Valhalla; talent was not a sufficient prerequisite for immortality. He needed genius and there was no assurance that he had it, no assurance that he had done anything more "than learned his lessons well."

Stephen's phrase irritated him, impinged itself upon his consciousness and bored in relentlessly. He was uncertain whether it had been meant to be an aphoristic jest or a sarcastic jibe. Was it a meaty phrase carrying the sting of an adder? Or was it a listless phrase coined to discourage further boring conversation? He did not know, and he had no insight into the machinery which had produced it. But he could not aerate it from his mind. Insistently it flashed across his brain, formed itself into flaming letters before his eyes, and dinned its searing way into his ears.

He soon came to the conclusion that he was cutting a ridiculous figure. On three distinct occasions now, twice with Stephen and once with Lucille, this unwelcome characterization had seemed apt in the light of what they had said on those occasions. He was a self-deluded posturer. A consummate jackass...

Walking through Central Park. Mind chaotic and deranged. Mind tortured, a seething melting pot into which too much unfiltered metal had been poured. Coherence was lacking. Ideas toppled over one another, ideas the result of wide reading and too hasty assimilation. His was an adolescent brain. It had not matured sufficiently to exercise caution and restraint. It had seized upon attractive brilliants, fed upon predigested cereals, and made no use of cauterizing gastric fluids. Yet there was something fundamental there striving for expression and relief, something which protested against unprincipled inundation and unprincipled expression-something which cautioned him to take inventory, and invite maturity.

Despite his superiority complex he was different from most people he knew, precociously different. The difficulty being that he was wont to pervert rather than to train and cultivate this difference. It was something to be paraded rather than something to be carefully nurtured. It was something to release halfcocked in order to shock rather than something to utilize essentially. There had been no catharsis, no intellectual metabolism. In pretending to be a dispenser of pearls to swine he had only proved that he, too, sometimes wallowed in the mire.

The struggle to free himself from race conscious ness had been hailed before actually accomplished.. The effort to formulate a new attitude toward life. had become a seeking for a red badge of courage. That which might have emerged normally, if given time, had been forcibly and prematurely exposed to the light. It now seemed as if the Caesarian operation was going to prove fatal both to the parent and to the child.

Futile introspection, desperate flagellations of self which still left him in darkness and despair.

On his way home Raymond tried hard to recall all the various items with which he had concerned himself. He had a confused recollection of having thought about innumerable subjects, innumerable people, but the thoughts were now nebulous and fast fading into obscurity, and there was no key to the dark labyrinth to which they had fled. He had no definite memories, no dominant conclusions. His day of solitude, his day of stock taking, had all been in vain.

Arriving home, he wearily climbed the exterior stone stairs and fumbled in his pocket for his door key. But before he could make use of it, the door was flung open and Paul, obviously excited, grabbed him by the arm, and pulled him into the hallway.

"Come upstairs quick."

Into the studio Paul rushed him. The door was eased shut. Aline and Stephen were sitting on the couch. Their faces were livid. Their eyes sparkled with excitement. They abruptly left their seats and rushed toward him.

"Pelham's been arrested."

"Been arrested?" Raymond echoed Aline's dramatic announcement. "For what?"

"We don't know," Paul spoke hurriedly before the others. "I just came in. Steve and Aline told me."

Raymond relaxed: "Nonsense."

"No foolin'," Stephen spoke for the first time. "They've taken him to jail."

"For what?" Raymond reiterated impatiently, his eyes beseeching Stephen for a satisfactory answer.

"Crimminy, we don't know. Aline and I were in his

room. He was doing our portrait again. The doorbell rang. He rushed downstairs and a moment later ushered two burly whites into the room. One of them asked if he was George Jones. He smiled blandly and said yes. The burly one flashed a star and said they had a warrant for his arrest. I was dumbfounded. Pelham gasped helplessly, completely in articulate. They ordered him to put on his coat and hat. He had on his smock and beret. Then they turned to Aline and me. Such belligerence. 'Are you white one of them roared. I answered yes. What aya doin' here?' he shouted again. As calmly as possible I said: 'Just visiting friends.' 'Is she white?' he roared again, pointing at Aline. I had presence of mind enough to say yes. I knew they could not tell the difference. Then they searched the room, looked under the bed, in all the drawers, and in Pelham's trunk. Their search finished, they led the stupefied Pelham from the room still attired in his mock and beret. That's all."

"But. . . " Raymond floundered. "What did you do? Did you call Euphoria?"

"She wasn't home, nor in her office. I've tried several times."

Raymond did not know what to do or say next. The whole affair was incomprehensible. There must be some mistake. He tried to review Pelham's recent activities. They were all innocent enough. He seldom left the house except to shop for groceries or accompany someone to the movies. There was nothing which Raymond could construe as criminal. It must all be a gross error.

"Hell," he exclaimed at last. "I'm going to the police station."

There was a precinct station only three blocks away. Raymond practically ran the entire distance, brushing people out of his way, recklessly rushing in front of speeding taxis. Finally he was standing breathless before an indifferent desk sergeant.

He gasped for sufficient breath to speak.

"Ha. . . have you got a Pelham Gaylord here?"

The sergeant's index finger searched the record book.

"No."

"Oh. . . I mean. . . George Jones."

The index finger was active again.

"Yes."

"What's he in for?" eagerly.

"Rape."

"Rape?" The echo was a shrill shout.

"Umhum."

There was a pause while Raymond sought to regain his poise and voice.

"Can I see him?"

"Naw. They'll arraign him in Washington Heights court tomorrow morning. You can see him after that."

The desk telephone rang. Raymond was dismissed. Completely puzzled and nonplussed he returned home.

The house was ablaze with lights. As he opened the door he heard a woman crying hysterically. He was too dazed by the sudden and incredulous turn of events to be more than mildly startled by this fresh development. Again Paul met him.

"Old Bernhardt's having hysterics." Bernhardt was their nickname for the actress lady who lived on the top floor. Raymond shrugged his shoulders and started up the stairs. He could not concern himself with the world's madness. From the third floor came the meaningless whines and screams of a temporarily deranged woman. Euphoria briskly de follow her into Pelham's studio. She shut the door when he had entered, leaving Paul on the outside.

"This is a hell of a mess."

"What?" Raymond queried inanely.

"Didn't you go to the jail?"

"Sure. But what's it all about?"

"Pelham raped Gladys." Gladys was the older of the actress lady's two daughters.

"Nonsense." He couldn't believe it.

"Read this." Euphoria pulled a piece of paper from her purse and handed it to him. It was a poem addressed "To

Gladys." Still incredulous, he plunged into the meticulously penned lines:

> *Oh you who I adore*
> *And do anything for*
> *Remember the song*
> *Entitled let's do it*
> *The bees and the birds*
> *All do it*
> *So why not you and me?*

Raymond sank into a nearby chair. His laughter was prolonged and contagious. Inquisitive Paul opened the door and stealthily slipped in. And in the room above, the distrait mother alternately shrieked, moaned, and paced the floor, then stopped abruptly to ascertain if there was any sign of an audience.

XV

At ten o'clock the next morning Raymond, Paul, Stephen, and Eustace met Euphoria at the Washington Heights court. The room was already crowded and they were unable to find seats near the front. Making themselves satisfied with what they found, they impatiently awaited the calling of Pelham's case.

The courtroom was compact and dreary. The electric lights on the sides of the wall and those depending from the ceiling did little to dispel the room's depressive gloom. Seedy proletarians of all races occupied the benches and chairs. A towering policeman with a flaming red face guarded the entrance door, professionally scrutinizing all who passed him Near the rear of the room was a railed in enclosure for the press and for lawyers. The judge's bench loomed in front of this, separated by a passageway, which led to a prisoners pen on the left and consultation rooms on the right.

A court stenographer and two clerks were seated at a table in front of the judge's throne. Three immaculate policemen stood at attention at spaced intervals along the passageway. The magistrate was at his post, strabismic, formidable. There was a deal of noise and chattering. Bail runners cluttered up the doorway leading to the prisoners' pen. A prisoner stood near the stenographer's table, flanked by a policeman, what appeared to be his lawyer, and three other men in civilian clothes. No one could distinguish what was being said. For five minutes there was a droning interchange, then the policemen led the prisoner back to the pen. The others sought one of the consultation rooms.

Five Negroes were led in next. A policeman read from a sheet of lined foolscap. Only an occasional word mounted the noise sufficiently to be heard. The complaining policeman then stepped forward and with many angry gestures stated his case. The judge said something to the men. Only one of them replied. The rest blasphemed the complaining officer with their eyes and facial expressions. The spokesman finished. The judge rapped his gavel and said "dismissed" in a loud voice, then directed a grumbling monologue at the crestfallen complaining officer. The Negroes were ushered past the lawyer's pew. They shuffled gleefully down the aisle and were soon out of the room. They were free.

The pageant continued. A wizened little Jew was the next culprit. There was a great hubbub his case was called. Numerous Negro women, most of whom were accompanied by small children, left their seats and advanced before the judge's dais. Euphoria opined that he was a landlord up for some infraction of the rent law or for failure to provide heat and hot water. The case was bitter and intense. There were times when more than six people were all shouting at the judge at the same time. He had great difficulty keeping order. It could be seen that he was becoming impatient, irascible. Finally he silenced all and delivered a scathing lecture. Everyone concerned was abashed and quiet when he had finished. The case proceeded with some semblance of order.

No matter how hard they tried, Pelham's friends were unable to hear more than an occasional word or phrase. There was much chattering among those around them. And through the open windows came the insistent roar of an air drill as it red through the stubborn granite cliffs in the subway excavation below the surface of the street.

After an hour of ceaseless activity and droning of voices, the group was finally aroused from its lethargy by seeing Pelham being led in by a policeman. He was still attired in his green smock. He carried his beret in his hand. He appeared to be frightened and dejected. His eyes darted about nervously. His black face glistened. He was indeed a pitiable, yet comic, figure, incongruously attired in studio clothes, timidly standing before the awesome spectacle of the judge, while a police clerk read from the inevitable foolscap. When this was finished, the judge was seen to speak. One of the policemen detached himself from the crowd and went to one of the consultation rooms on the right. Opening the door he beckoned to someone inside. Almost immediately a woman juvenile officer emerged, followed by the actress lady and her allegedly defiled daughter.

The procession arranged itself in front of the judge's bench. The actress lady was weeping. The girl stood by, an awkward adolescent, bewildered and frightened. There was much interchange of talk, then the judge looked out over the lawyer's pew and made an announcement. A saffron young elegant answered this summons, advanced to the front, and halted beside the quaking Pelham. There was much more talk, and many hysterical outbursts on the part of the actress lady who held the spotlight and starred throughout the entire proceedings. Finally it was over. Pelham was led to the prisoners' pen, furtively wiping his eyes and cheeks with his black beret. The policewoman led the silent girl and her weeping mother back into the consultation room. The saffron elegant and the lineup of police and detectives dissolved in the crowd. A new group appeared. The pageant was continuing.

Raymond led the way out of the courtroom. His companions followed him into the street, silent, perplexed, knowing no more than they had on the night before.

XVI

Everyone assembled in Raymond's studio as usual that evening. Raymond took up a collection and sent Paul out for gin and ginger ale. Eustace in the inevitable green dressing gown stalked the open spaces of the room, spouting puns, humming spirituals. Stephen was pre-occupied and gruff. He continually pushed Aline away from him and when she insisted upon putting her arms around his neck, abruptly left his usual seat on the daybed and sat on the floor beside the surprised Janet. Aline in a huff perched herself jealously on the arm of the wicker chair to which Raymond was seemingly rooted. Bull and Lucille occupied the other wicker chair, wrapped in one another's arms.

They were all waiting for Euphoria. She had gone to consult the saffron elegant, who it seemed was her attorney and had been sent by her to defend the luckless Pelham. Until she returned their ignorance of details concerning Pelham's case was abysmal and irritating.

Paul returned with three quarts of gin and an equal amount of pale dry ginger ale. He placed his bundles on the table in the alcove and sauntered back into the room, taking his usual place on the floor. Simultaneously it occurred to almost everyone in the room that Pelham was not present to mix the drinks. All eyes focused themselves on Paul, but he ignored their silent request and fumbled for a match with which to light his cigarette. Raymond slumped deeper into his chair. Stephen yawned. Bull scowled. Eustace stopped his meandering.

"What ho! No ganymede? Guess I'll have to drix the minks." He plunged into the alcove and began his task, humming, *All God's Chilluns Got Wings* the while.

Conversation was desultory until after the fourth round of drinks and was stimulated then only because Paul happened to twit Eustace about his unpredictable range of voice.

"Your voice is changing."

WALLACE THURMAN

"Changing?"

"Um hum, second childhood. It goes up and down."

"That was the song, idiot, not my voice."

"Have it your way."

Eustace was exasperated. He turned to Raymond:

"Why will Paul discuss things about which he knows nothing? He's always talking about my voice and he knows nothing about music."

"I know I like Debussy better than Strauss. That George Antheil is a genius and that Ravel is in finitely superior to Schubert."

"Preposterous," Eustace made a deprecating gesture. "There are no modern musicians worthy of a seat beside Schubert."

"Here, here," Stephen interpolated. "You're a bloody blue stocking."

"I know music."

"Oh, yeah! I suppose that's why you sang a hymn by Handel and told Pelham it was an exercise by Brahms." Paul's voice was crooningly sarcastic. Everyone laughed except Bull who continued to scowl and Eustace who pulled the cord of his dressing gown more tightly about his waist, and enunciated in his most freezing manner:

"I never argue with ignorance. Let's dake another trink." Then visibly amused by his own witty victory, he began to collect the empty glasses, belligerently singing softly to himself all the while.

There was a knock at the door and Euphoria was in the room. She threw her hat on the table and leaned against the door.

"What's up?" Raymond inquired for all. Euphoria took a deep breath.

"Well, the sap's in for it."

"Did he really rape her?" Stephen still could not believe it.

"He says he didn't. And the doctor says there is no evidence that this is the first time she's been tampered with."

"The hussy," Eustace muttered disdainfully.

"They can't hold him, then," Raymond was hopeful.

"They are holding him," Paul reminded him impertinently.

"And they're going to hold him for trial. He's sunk. You ought to see the stuff he's written her. It's awful." She ran her words wearily together.

"Was it signed?" Lucille asked.

"No, but she proved it was his handwriting."

"How?"

"Well, she had him write her a special poem. She had found the other stuff. And with his signed poem she hastened to the police station."

"Well, I'll be damned," Stephen gasped, as did Paul and Raymond. They all remembered how faithfully Pelham had worked on that poem because the lady was appreciative and anxious to help him gain public honor and prestige.

"Ay God, the girl was clever. Sorry I can't say as much for Pelham. But why such Machiavellian tactics? Being true to her art, I suppose." Stephen mused more to himself than to the others in the room.

"He oughta go to jail and stay there," Bull growled. "What the hell's he messin' with a minor for? They oughta give him life."

"Can't," Lucille spoke quickly. "There's really not proof he actually raped her, is there?"

"Wait'll you hear the stuff he wrote her. Maybe he didn't rape her, but there has been some sort of relationship and you must remember she's under the age of consent. I didn't know he was such an imbecile. I got to see him at the Tombs. He cried all the time I was there and swore he hadn't harmed her. I asked him why he wrote her such stuff. Said he was trying to write like Paul."

"Good God!" Paul gasped. "Such blasphemy."

Euphoria continued.

"Pat, the lawyer, saw the poems in prose. They were the worst. Talked about kissing her in secret places and churning butter in the lily cup."

That is plagiarism, eh, Paul?" Stephen inquired, then quoted from memory:

"Your body is an index of uncut leaves
Which my searing kisses will burn apart,
An elusive packet of lilies churned
By love to make perfume."

"Yours was bad enough. I'd love to see Pelham's. But can't they see," he grew serious, "that it's only what he thinks is poetry."

"In the past tense, old dear, with remarks to the effect of what had happened and how much more enjoyable it would be in the future once she had the hang of it. One to three years is what he'll get."

Everyone sobered except Paul, who advanced consolingly: "Well, at least we'll have a trial to go to."

"Heartless wretch." Lucille glared at him.

"Well," he made a fanciful gesture with his left hand, "there is nothing we can do about it and I've always wanted to see someone I know on trial."

"Why don't you take Pelham's place?" Eustace suggested.

"First of all, I haven't raped anyone, and, secondly, I wouldn't be so commonplace. When I go on trial. . . "

"Which will be soon," Eustace persisted. Paul ignored the interruption. "It will be in the grand manner like Wilde or Villon or Dostoievsky's near execution. You see, I'm a genius." And he sipped contentedly from his half empty glass.

XVII

Raymond looked up from his book and smiled a greeting as Stephen entered the room.

"'Lo, stranger. Where've you been?"

"Oh. . . nowhere."

"Nowhere," Raymond laughed. "He stays away all night and half the next day and has been nowhere. Extraordinary."

"It really doesn't matter, does it?"

Raymond frowned and closed his book.

"What the hell's the matter with you, Steve?"

"Nothing."

"You're a liar. Ever since the night Pelham was arrested, you've been acting like a fool. Spit it out."

Stephen vouchsafed no reply. He merely lit a cigarette and crouched low in one of the wicker chairs.

Raymond regarded his friend steadily. For some time now he had been aware of a definite change in Stephen's manner. It had been apparent, as he had just said, from the night of Pelham's arrest, and had seemed to grow more pronounced as time passed.

He was always, it seemed, excessively preoccupied with some personal matter about which he was most secretive and depressed. He seldom as of yore began a conversation, and his only contribution to those begun by others was invariably succinct and gruff. It had been noticed by everyone with whom he came into frequent contact. All had remarked upon his protracted surliness and unusual silence. And Raymond had become sensitively aware of how his friend sat among a crowd, tense, aloof, wary, steadily eyeing each and every individual as if suspicious of some contemplated overt action. Raymond was frankly worried, especially when he noted that Stephen was even evading him, craftily escaping from *tête-à-têtes*, deliberately foiling every effort Raymond made to indulge in one of their usual gabfests.

"Steve," Raymond advanced after a period of re flection,

WALLACE THURMAN

"you've got to tell me what's wrong."

"Jesus Christ. Can't a fellow be tired and moody?"

"Certainly, but that's not all. I've seen you tired. and moody before."

"All right then. . . you're the doctor. Treat yourself to a diagnosis."

"Perhaps if you'd be more frank I could."

"Aw, dry up. . . will you?"

Raymond said nothing more at the moment, but his mind remained active. What could be wrong with his friend? One answer suggested itself to him, but he dismissed it immediately and let a more improbable one replace it.

It was, perhaps, the result of Stephen's recent hectic relationship with Aline and Janet. Raymond remembered how Stephen, on the night following Pelham's arraignment, had abruptly deserted Aline and turned to Janet. This gesture had occasioned much speculation, for everyone knew of the rivalry which existed between the two for Stephen's favors. It had become a community joke which Stephen himself had suddenly squelched for a while by deliberately avoiding Janet and confining his caresses to Aline alone.

And then, when even Janet had begun to accept her defeat stoically. Stephen had precipitated con fusion by vacillating from one to the other like a self-controlled automaton. Janet one night. . .

Aline the next. The situation had become comically serious, and because both of the girls invariably confided in Raymond, he had come to bear the brunt of the nervous strain.

The two girls, hitherto inseparable, despite frequent outbursts of temper such as had followed Janet's confession to Raymond sometime before, had now developed a positive dislike for one another. Recriminations and harsh words curdled their every moment together. A pitched battle seemed imminent. In vain had Raymond called a peace conference and tried to make them see that Stephen alone was to blame.

The prize was too valuable to relinquish without a fight,

and the vanity of the combatants had been pricked to the bleeding point. It was to be a war until one or the other emerged completely victorious with disposition of the booty settled once and for all.

The situation had become surfeited with complications. Janet was preparing to move away from Aline's house. Each had begun telling the state secrets of the other. It was obvious that only a mere gesture was needed to set off fatal fireworks. Raymond appealed to Stephen. And Stephen immediately settled the whole matter by beginning completely to ignore the two of them.

The new régime, too, had been difficult, but it had at least served to lessen hostilities between the two combatants. Instead of reviling one another, they now joined forces to break down Stephen's reserve and antagonism. But the object of their affections remained aloof, polite, cold, as if only minutely aware either of their existence or any past relationship.

It was this comic interlude which Raymond had sought to blame for the change in Stephen, but he was not convinced by his own reasoning, for he knew that Aline and Janet had been but superficial bagatelles in Stephen's life. He had enjoyed toying with them, enjoyed playing them one against the other. Their emotional reactions to him had been something to observe and analyze. The physical pleasure they had afforded him had been enjoyable, but of no particular consequence. Emotionally, Stephen had not been involved at all.

There was then something else... but... the something else which kept insinuating itself into Raymond's mind seemed too preposterous and complex to be recognized or considered.

"Steve," Raymond spoke suddenly, having decided upon a new line of attack, "I found something of yours today." He pulled several sheets of paper from between the pages of the book he had been reading. "I think it's well written but slightly cock eyed. Do you remember it?" He handed the sheets to his friend.

Stephen cast a cursory glance at the first page, smiled contemptuously, briefly, then calmly tore the sheets in half.

"What's the idea? I wanted to save that."

"For what?"

Raymond was piqued. His annoyance carried over into his tone of voice.

"Because it interested me, of course."

"You're nuts," Stephen replied and proceeded to tear the paper into smaller bits. "All trash, son. All trash. *My* first impressions of Harlem. Transparent juvenilia. Alice in Wonderland, myopic, color-blind, deaf."

Raymond said nothing. He feared to intrude upon his friend's muttered confidences. Perhaps Stephen would continue and at last reveal his true state of mind. Raymond leaned forward expectantly. Stephen started to speak, but whatever he was about to say remained unspoken, for at that precise moment, Paul and Eustace bounded merrily into the room.

"We got it. We got it," they shouted in unison, and holding hands performed a ridiculous ring-a round the rosy in the center of the room.

"You've got what?" Raymond queried angrily.

"Wouldn't you like to know? An' I mean it's hot stuff. . . eh, Eustace?"

They continued their senseless prancing. Stephen abruptly left his chair, jammed his hat onto his head, and started for the door.

"Nay, nay, milord," Eustace barred his way. "List ye to the revelation. Tell 'em, Paul."

"Gentlemen," Paul made a mock bow, "having considered the scarceness of food in our cupboard, Eustace and I went into a huddle and held a seance. The spirits were kind enough to reveal to us a plan whereby we can thwart the wolf. We're going to give a donation party."

"A what?" Raymond growled.

"A donation party. We'll invite everyone we know and those we don't. The price of admission will be groceries. Isn't that grand?"

Stephen muttered something under his breath, pushed the jubilant Eustace aside, and left the room. The door was viciously slammed. He could be heard stomping down the stairs.

"Mercy," Eustace exclaimed, "my nerves! What's wrong with him?"

"Ah, let him go," Paul said. "Aren't you for our party, Ray?"

"I'm for any damn thing. But for Christ's sake, get the hell out of here and leave me alone." No one moved. "Didn't you hear me say get out? Now scram."

He stretched out on the bed, face downward. A moment later the door was slammed again, and there was the soft swish of silk as Eustace followed Paul down the stairs.

XVIII

It was the night of the Donation Party. For ten days preparations had been made. For ten days Raymond's typewriter and the telephone had been overworked, bidding people to report to Niggeratti Manor on the designated night. The wolf must be driven from the door. Paul had scuttled through Greenwich Village, a jubilant Revere, sounding the tocsin. Euphoria and Eustace had canvassed their Harlem friends. Barbara had been called in for a consultation and departed ebullient, a zealous crusader. A large crowd had been assured. The audacious novelty of the occasion had piqued many a curiosity. And of course there was promise of uninhibited hijinks.

Ten o'clock. Only a few guests had arrived, laden with various bundles of staple foods. Eustace's studio and the nearby kitchen were to be the focal points for the party because in the basement there would be fewer stairs for the drunks to encounter, and more room for dancing.

Ten-thirty. The Niggeratti clique, supplemented by a few guests, had gathered around the punch bowl on the kitchen table. The concoction, fathered by Eustace, was tasty and strong.

"Ol' Mother Savoy has surpassed herself to night," Paul murmured between drinks.

Also on the table were a half dozen bottles of gin, and Raymond noted that it was to one of these that Stephen was clinging tenaciously.

"Have some punch?"

"No," Stephen answered Raymond shortly and continued to gulp down glass after glass of straight gin.

"Go easy, Steve. The night's young."

"What of it?" He walked away from the table and leaned against the wall in a far corner of the room.

Before Raymond had time to consider his friend's unusual behavior, a host of people boisterously invaded the room, dropping packages, clamoring for drinks.

"Two cans of corn," someone shouted.

"Pound of sugar here. "

"Some yaller corn meal. Hot ziggitty,"

"Taters! Taters. Nice ripe 'taters."

"Wet my whistle, Eustace. I lithp."

Samuel emerged from the crowd and taking hold of Raymond's arm pulled him aside. It was the first time they had met since their quarrel some weeks before. Samuel was contrite, anxious for a reconciliation. He had reasoned to himself that he had been too quick to lose his temper. People like him—people with a mission in life—must expect to be the recipients of insults and rebuffs. How could he help others when he could not control himself? Samuel felt that he had betrayed his purpose in life by reacting positively to Raymond's drunken statements.

"Ray, I owe you an apology."

"For what?"

"For what happened."

"Oh, that. Forget it." Raymond turned away and rejoined the exuberant crowd centered around the kitchen table.

"Ray." It was Paul. "Meet a friend of mine."

By his side was a grinning black boy.

"Ray, this is Bud. He's a bootblack, but he has the most beautiful body I've ever seen. I'll get him to strip for the gang soon."

The boy grinned sheepishly. But he did not seem the least bit abashed. Before Raymond could make any comment, Paul had propelled his charge toward Eustace's studio. Raymond followed. The room was crowded with people. Black people, white people, and all the in-between shades. Ladies in evening gowns. Ladies in smocks. Ladies in tailored suits. Ladies in ordinary dresses of every description, interspersed and surrounded by all types of men in all types of conventional clothes. And weaving his way among them, green dressing gown swishing, glass tray held tightly in both hands, was Eustace, serving drinks to those who had not yet found the kitchen oasis.

"Folks," Paul shouted above the din, "this is Bud. He has the most perfect body in New York. I'm gonna let you see it soon."

"Bravo."

"Go to it."

"Now?"

Paul and his protégé were surrounded by an avid mob.

Raymond sauntered back into the kitchen. Stephen was still standing in his isolated corner, a full glass progressing toward his lips. His face was flushed. His eyes half closed. Raymond started toward him.

"Hi, Ray." Someone jerked the tail of his coat. It was Bull. Beside him was Lucille.

"Hen's fruit." Bull deposited a sack full of eggs on top of the refrigerator.

"Eve's delight." A bag of apples was thrust into Raymond's hand by some unknown person.

"An' my sweet patootie has the bacon," Bull continued, jerking an oblong package from beneath Lucille's arm. Raymond put the apples beside Bull's

"Hello, 'Cile. Thanks, Bull."

"Oh, Ray." It was Barbara. She was followed and surrounded by a group of detached, anemic white men and women, all in evening dress, all carrying packages of various sizes and shapes.

"This is Ray, folks," Barbara announced to her companions. They all smiled dutifully and began relieving themselves of their bundles.

Barbara appropriated Raymond's hand and placed something in his palm.

"For Negro art," she whispered, then, slipping quickly away, corralled her friends and ushered them toward the punch bowl. Raymond opened his palm and gasped at the sight of a twenty-dollar bill.

"Good God, what a mob." Lucille was beside him. He pocketed the money Barbara had given him and regarded

Lucille coolly.

"Still hep on your man?"

"Why, Ray," she began, then quickly regaining control of herself, riposted merrily, "and *how*." She then started to move away.

Raymond forestalled her by firmly clenching her wrist in his hand.

"How long you gonna play this game?" he asked sternly.

"What ol' black game?"

"You know damn well.

"Here's a drink, baby." Bull handed Lucille a glass of punch. Raymond released her wrist, glared at the two of them, walked to the table, pushed his way through the crowd, seized a glass, and handed it to Euphoria, now guardian of the punch bowl, to fill.

After having had several drinks, he threaded his way back into Eustace's studio. It was more crowded and noisy than before. Someone was playing the piano, and in a small clearing the ex-wife of a noted American playwright was doing the Black Bottom with a famed Negro singer of spirituals.

"Ain't I good?" she demanded of her audience. "An' you ain't seen nothin' yet."

With which she insinuated her scrawny white body close to that of her stalwart black partner and began performing the torrid abdominal movements of the "mess-a-round."

"How d'y'do, Ray."

Raymond turned to see who had spoken. On the davenette against the wall was a well-known sophisticated author and explorer of the esoteric. He was surrounded by four bewildered-looking, corn-fed individuals. He introduced them to Raymond as relatives and friends from his native middle west. It was their first trip to Harlem, and their first experience of a white-black gathering.

Raymond sat down beside them, talking at random, and helping himself to the bottles of liquor which the cautious author had recruited from his own private stock.

Soon there was a commotion at the door. It cleared of

all standees, and in it was framed the weird Amazonian figure of Amy Douglas, whose mother had made a fortune devising and marketing hair preparations for kinky-haired blackamoors. Amy, despite her bulk and size—she was almost six feet tall and weighed over two hundred pounds—affected flimsy frocks and burdened her person with weighty brilliants. A six months stay in Europe had provided her with a series of foreign phrases with which to interlard her southern dialect. Being very black, she went in for skin whiteners which had been more effective in certain spots than in others. As a result, her face was speckled, uncertain of its shade. Amy was also generous in the use of her mother's hair preparations, and because someone had once told her she resembled a Nubian queen, she wore a diamond tiara, precariously perched on the top of her slickened naps.

Majestically she strode into the room, attended as usual by an attractive escort of high yaller ladies in waiting, and a chattering group of effeminate courtiers.

Raymond excused himself from the people with whom he had been sitting and started once more for the kitchen. While trying to pierce through the crowd, he was halted by Dr. Parkes, a professor of literature in a northern Negro college, who, also, as Paul so aptly declared, played mother hen to a brood of chicks, he having appointed himself guardian angel to the current set of younger Negro artists.

"I've been trying to find you for the past hour."

"Sorry, Dr. Parkes. . . but in this mob. . . "

"I know. Perhaps I should await a more propitious moment, but I wanted to ask you about Pelham."

"Pelham?"

"Yes.

"Oh, he's still in jail. That's all I know. His trial isn't far off. I've forgotten the exact date."

"What effect do you think this will have on you?"

"On me? I don't know what you mean."

"Don't you think this scandal when publicized will hurt all of you who lived here with Pelham?"

Raymond laughed.

"I hadn't thought of that. This might be Paul's opportunity to get his name in the paper."

"Who's taking my name in vain?" Paul appeared, still leading his dark shadow by the hand. "Oh, Dr. Parkes," he continued excitedly, "meet Bud. He's got. . ."

Raymond escaped and worked his way over to the piano. He stopped to chat with Aline and Janet, who had staggered in some time before with a group of conspicuously and self-consciously drunk college boys.

"Hi, Ray."

"What say, keeds?"

"Where's Steve?" they asked in unison.

"Find the gin," he replied and moved away.

Meanwhile four Negro actors from a current Broadway dramatic hit harmonized a popular love song. Conversation was temporarily hushed, laughter subsided, and only the intermittent tinkle of ice in an upturned glass could be heard as the plangent voices of the singers filled the room.

There was a burst of applause as they finished, followed by boisterous calls for an encore. After a moment's conference, the singers obligingly crooned another mellifluous tune.

Raymond retraced his steps, greeting people, whispering answers to questions buzzed into his ear. Finally he was once more in the kitchen.

It was one-thirty. The twenty dollar bill had been given to Eustace, who had sent for another dozen bottles of gin. A deposed Russian countess was perched atop the gas range talking animatedly in broken English to Paul's Spartan bootblack. The famed American playwright's ex-wife had developed a crying jag. No one could soothe her but the stalwart singer of Negro spirituals. Near them hovered his wife, jealous, bored, suspicious, irritated rather than flattered by the honeyed, Oxonian witticisms being cooed into her ear by a drunken English actor.

The noise was deafening. Empty gin bottles on the floor tripped those with unsteady legs. Bull's bag of eggs had been knocked to the floor. Its con rents were broken and oozed stickily over the linoleum. Someone else had dropped a bag of sugar. The linoleum was gritty. Shuffling feet made rasping sounds.

Two-thirty. Raymond began to feel the effects of the liquor he had consumed. He decided to stop drinking for a while. There was too much to see to risk missing it by getting drunk.

In the hallway between the kitchen and Eustace's studio, Euphoria sought to set a group of Negro schoolteachers at ease. The crowd confused them as it did most of the Harlem intellectuals who had strayed in and who all felt decidedly out of place. Raymond noticed how they all clung together, how timid they were, and how constrained they were in conversation and manner. He sought Stephen. He wanted to share his amusement at their discomfiture and self-consciousness. It gave him pleasure that he should have such a pertinent example of their lack of social savoir, their race conscious awareness. Unable to recover from being so intimately surrounded by whites, they, the schoolteachers, the college boys, the lawyers, the dentists, the social service workers, despite their strident appeals for social equality when among their own kind, either communed with one another, standing apart, or else made themselves obnoxious striving to make themselves agreeable. Only the bootblack, the actors, the musicians and Raymond's own group of friends comprised the compatible Negroid elements,

This suggested a formal train of thought to Raymond's mind. Ignoring all those who called to him. he sought for Stephen. But Stephen was nowhere to be found, either in the kitchen, or in the studio where some unidentified russet brown girl was doing a cooch dance to a weird piano accompaniment.

Raymond made a tour of the house, surprised many amorous couples in the darkened rooms upstairs by turning on the light, disturbed the fanciful aggregation of Greenwich Village uranians Paul had gathered in Raymond's studio to admire his bootblack's touted body, and irritated and annoyed two snarling women who had closeted themselves in the bathroom, but still Stephen was not to be found.

Disconsolately, Raymond discontinued his search and returned to the main scene of the party. All were convivial and excited. Various persons sang and danced. Highballs were quickly disposed of. A jazz pianist starred at the piano. There was a rush to dance. Everyone seemed to be hilariously drunk. Shouts of joy merged into one persistent noisy blare. Couples staggered from the kitchen to the studio and back again. Others leaned despairingly, sillily against the walls, THE SPRING or else sank helplessly into chairs or windowsills. Fresh crowds continued to come in. The Donation Party was successful beyond all hopes.

Raymond felt a tug on his arm. It was Samuel. His face was flushed. His eyes were angry. Raymond tried to elude him.

"I've got to talk to you, Ray." He held tightly to Raymond's arm.

"Wait till tomorrow. Who in the hell can talk with all this noise?"

"But you don't know what's happened!"

"And I don't give a good..."

"Listen, Ray, for God's sake," Samuel interrupted. "Find Steve and get him out of here. He's terribly drunk and in an awful mess."

"What the hell are you talking about?"

"He, Aline and Janet just had a scrap."

"Where is he?"

"I don't know, Ray. No one can find him. He was standing in the door there... to Eustace's place. All at once there was a great confusion. I pushed through the crowd just in time to hear Steve shout: 'You goddamn sluts.' And before I could grab him, he had hit Janet in the face, took a punch at Aline and rushed away."

"Oh Jesus, Which way did he go?"

"Out the front door."

The two of them forged their way through the crowd and went out into the street. Without a word they raced to the end of the block, peeped into the speakeasy, then glanced down the intersecting thorough fare. Stephen was nowhere in sight.

"See what you've done," Samuel shouted. "You've got a decent boy into a sordid mess. I told him not to live with niggers. I knew what'd happen."

But Raymond heard not one word of his tirade, for he had rushed away from Samuel, and run back to the house alone.

The party had reached new heights. The lights in the basement had been dimmed, and the reveling dancers cast grotesque shadows on the heavily tapestried walls. Color lines had been completely eradicated. Whites and blacks clung passionately together as if trying to effect a permanent merger. Liquor, jazz music, and close physical contact had achieved what decades of propaganda had advocated with little success.

Here, Raymond thought, as he continued his search for Stephen, is social equality. Tomorrow all of them will have an emotional hangover. They will fear for their sanity, for at last they have had a chance to do openly what they only dared to do clandestinely before. This, he kept repeating to himself, is the Negro renaissance, and this is about all the whole damn thing is going to amount to.

Stephen was nowhere to be found. Nor were Aline or Janet or anyone else who might tell him what had happened. Raymond felt nauseated. The music, the noise, the indiscriminate lovemaking, the drunken revelry began to sicken him. The insanity of the party, the insanity of its implications, threatened his own sanity. It is going to be necessary, he thought, to have another emancipation to deliver the emancipated Negro from a new kind of slavery.

He made his way to the kitchen, rejoined the crowd around the punch bowl, and, for the next hour or more, drank incontinently. He grew drunker by the moment. He had a faint idea that Euphoria was dragging him aside and telling him that the noise must be toned down, and that there must be no more brawls, or bawdy parties in the bedrooms. The next thing he remembered was snatching Lucille away from some unidentified man, and dragging her viciously into the pantry.

"Y' want a cave man, eh?" he shouted. All else was vague and jumbled. Five minutes later he passed quietly out on the pantry floor.

Noon the next day found Eustace and Paul, still in pajamas, forgetting their hangovers, and impervious to the littered kitchen, taking inventory of the party's material gains. There were sacks of rice, potatoes, sugar, carrots, corn meal, flour, fruit, beans, black-eyed peas and string beans. There were cans of corn, peas, tomatoes, pineapple, fruit salad, soup, salmon, crab meat, lobster, caviar, shredded chicken, soups of all flavors, spaghetti, pork and beans, pimentoes. There were wafers, cheese crackers, soda biscuits and graham crackers. And, as a final touch, a half case of champagne, several quarts of burgundy, sauterne, port, chartreuse and dago red.

"Jesus master, look at this," Eustace kept shouting as he discovered item after item which would tickle his sensitive palate.

"Let's open the champagne," Paul urged eagerly. "Not till Ray gets up and we've cleaned up some of this mess. Euphoria's hoppin' mad as it is."

"Stoo bad Pelham ain't here. We could sure use him now,"

"I say, we could." The doorbell rang.

"Go get it, Paul. Maybe it's somebody come to help clean up."

Paul went to the door, and when he returned he carried a special delivery letter for Raymond.

"It's from Steve," he announced. "I recognize the handwriting."

"We'd better wake Ray up then, the drunken louse. Have you ever in your born days seen two people get as high as they did last night? And both of them got fighting drunks on at that. If I hadn't dragged poor Lucille out of the pantry, I'm sure Ray would've raped her. And what Steve did to Janet's nose."

"You wasn't so sober yourself, if it's any news to you."

"I may not have been sober but my love didn't come down like yours did."

"Passion, my dear Eustace, is much headier and more necessary to the artist than wine."

"Sez you. Come on, let's take this letter to Ray."

They went to Raymond's studio. He lay fully dressed on the top of his daybed, uncovered, sound asleep. They awoke him with difficulty.

"It's a letter from Steve," Paul explained. Immediately Raymond became fully awake. Snatching the letter from Paul's hand, he hastily tore open the envelope, and while his two friends stood by mystified, expectant, he read to himself:

Dear Ray:

I'm gone. Don't ask why. I can't stand it any longer. That party last night finished me. I've drunk my fill of Harlem. What that tokens for you and me, I don't know yet. I've wanted to break away for almost two weeks, but I didn't have the courage. It took Aline and Janet to finish me up for good. I couldn't seem to talk to you about it. I knew you would understand, but it all seemed so silly that I couldn't bring myself to discuss it.

I'm fed up on Harlem and on Negroes. You say there is nothing to this race business. In the past have agreed. Now I wonder. Dubiety surges through me and tantalizes my mind. I have no prejudices you know; yet recently my being has been permeated with a vague disquiet. I feel lost among Negroes. Of course, you know my opinion of the usual run of whites who go in for Harlem. I saw in myself a suggestion of that and it sickened me. But that's minor the major thing is not my dis quiet, but my growing dislike and antipathy. I shudder—and this will astound you—if I have to shake hands with a Negro. I have lived recently in a suddenly precipitated fear that I had become unclean because of my association. So complex and far reaching has this fear become that I rushed in a panic to a doctor recently to be examined. I feared, unreasonably, and with no definite evidence, that Aline and Janet were unclean and that I had become contaminated, diseased. I never thought positively about venereal diseases before, but even the doctor's reassuring Wassermann failed to allay my suspicions.

I'm a damned neurotic. I've been lording it over you and, god's teeth, I, too, am an egregious ass. All of your friends nauseate me. They are extremely pretentious and stupid. To have been surrounded by such a collection of whites would have driven me mad long ago. To have been surrounded by your friends without you would have been equally impossible. The thing, you see, is hopelessly entangled and the explanation, right as it is, is too simple for facile expression.

I am reminded again that the greatest phrase ever written is "words, words, words."

Mind, there are numerous things I hate in you (hate is advisedly used), but they are excrescences on the essential you that dovetail into the essential me. You stand apart from the others in Harlem, whom I can only describe as being festering gum boils. I can stomach them no longer. And I've gone away as you too should go. I have a room at the enclosed address. You can bring me my clothes. I can't come back but I must see you. . . and talk. It will get us nowhere, but maybe you'll see the light and have compassion. My phobia has become so pronounced that I automatically changed my seat in the subway last night when a Negro man sat down beside me.

You think it strange then that I should want to see and talk to you? But it isn't, however garbled and psychopathic it seems. You never have been and never will be a Negro to me. You're just you. But again words repeated three times. Note the 'phone number. I await your call.

Until then,
Steve

Raymond pocketed the letter quickly.

"What's happened to the goddamned Swede?"

Paul inquired. "Nothing." Raymond responded curtly and without another word got up, opened the door, ushered them out of the room, and was soon busy at his typewriter.

My dear Steve:

A messenger boy will bring your clothes. I do not care to see you just yet. I cannot see that any good can come out of it. There would surely be a gulf between us of your own making which would be difficult to bridge.

I am not angry, only surprised and a trifle chagrined that you felt it necessary to slip away without confiding in me.

I most certainly do understand your phobia and its accompanying reactions. God knows I too have experienced similar lunacies. This environment is enough to provoke almost any type of mental or physical malady. It is much easier for you to flee than for me. You know I'm not a social creature in the accepted sense of the word. I cannot bear to associate with the ordinary run of people. I have to surround myself with individuals, unusual

individuals who for the most part are more than
a trifle insane. Unless buttressed by stimulating
personalities, I am lost, no matter how despicable or
foolish those personalities may appear in retrospect.
They are the life of me. And unable to find many
people who, like you, stimulate me intellectually,
people with companionate minds (you know
how scarce they are in my world), I am forced to
surround myself with case studies in order not
completely to curdle and sour.

Your trouble can frankly be diagnosed as this:
your difference in color, as I have warned, has
been impressed upon you. Your distaste has been
externally administered. To be pedestaled and
fawned over is nauseating to any sensible being, to
become a pale god in a black world rests equally
foul upon the mind and stomach of a person
of your type. You want me to believe that some
dormant racial antipathy has been aroused in
your Nordic breast. Were that true it would not
be necessary for you to retain your affection and
mental affinity for me. I, too, would be flung on
the dung heap, a stinking carcass not to be suffered.
Maybe I am. Maybe you are just testing yourself
in wanting to see me again. Then, perhaps, you are
right after all, and our friendship may be a catalytic
agent conjoining two incompatible elements.
However, seek your balance. A few days temperance,
a few days meditation and sane living, a change of
scene, may work wonders.

Meanwhile, I wonder about the "excrescences on
the essential me."

Always,
Ray

Raymond reread the letter he had written, then addressed an envelope and prepared it for mailing. This done, he unlocked his door and going to the head of the stairs called Paul.

"Wha chu want?"

"Help me pack Steve's clothes."

"Pack his clothes?"

"That's what I said. And don't ask any fool questions."

They had just finished their task and called for a messenger boy when the doorbell rang. Eustace admitted Dr. Parkes and Samuel. He ushered them into Raymond's studio, excused himself, and ordered Paul to follow him to the kitchen. When they had gone, and the visitors were comfortably seated, Dr. Parkes cleared his throat and began to talk.

"Samuel and I have been discussing you."

Raymond anticipated what was to follow. His manner was by no means conducive to further con versation.

"Your interest is appreciated, I'm sure."

"Now don't misunderstand," Samuel spoke hurriedly. "We may seem to be taking liberties with your personal affairs, but you'll understand, won't you, that we are your friends?"

Raymond laughed. "What crime have I committed now?"

"None at all, none at all," Dr. Parkes clucked professionally in his best campus manner. "We just think it best that you move."

"Move?" Raymond had not been prepared for this.

"Yes. You see, it's like this. The newspapers here in Harlem are bound to make a sensation out of Pelham's case. They'll embroil you in it and all who come here."

"Nonsense. None of us have been mentioned, nor are any of us going to be called for witnesses when his trial comes up."

"It's not that entirely," Samuel proceeded. "It's that the house is getting a bad reputation. Did you see this editorial in the *New York Call*?"

He pulled a clipping from his pocket and handed it to Raymond. The *New York Call* was Harlem's most respectable news weekly. The editorial was typical of its columns. There was, it went on to say, a house in Harlem which had for its residents a number of young Negro writers and artists. Instead of pursuing their work, they were spending their time drinking and carousing with a low class of whites from downtown. Racial integrity they had none. They were satisfied to woo decadence, satisfied to dedicate their life to a routine of drunken ness and degeneracy with cheap white people, rather than mingle with the respectable elements of their own race. This showed of course in their work, which was, almost without exception, a glorification of the lowest strata of Negro life. Led on by their white friends, they were pandering to a current demand for the sensational, libeling their own people, injuring them, insulting them by being concerned only with Jezebels, pimps and other underworld fauna. Thus they aided and abetted those whites who would have the world believe that the Negro was an inferior, worthless creature, not capable of appreciating or indulging in the better things in life. Should this be allowed to continue? No. These young people should be brought to their senses.

They should be made to realize the futility and dan ger of the path they had chosen, the rosy path to hell. They should be taken aside and reasoned with, then if this failed the white light of publicity should be shed upon their activities and their innate vicious ness and duplicity exposed to the world.

Raymond laughed as he finished reading.

"Surely you don't take this tripe seriously?"

"It's not a matter of taking it seriously," Dr. Parkes answered solemnly. "It's a matter of protecting yourself from unnecessary attacks on your reputation. This is a new day in the history of our race. Talented Negroes are being watched by countless people, white and black, to produce something new, something tremendous. They are waiting for you to prove yourselves worthy so that they can help you. Scandal stories in the newspapers certainly won't influence the public favorably."

"My habits and life are my own business. I intend to live

just as I please, regardless of yellow journalism, or a public which might offer me mate rial aid should I, in their opinion, prove myself worthy." Raymond's words were crisp and angry.

"But you owe it. . . " Samuel began.

"I don't owe anything to anyone except myself."

Dr. Parkes made a final effort.

"But I'm afraid you don't understand. That party last night, for instance. Suppose the white press should take up this business of whites and Negroes mingling so indiscriminately and drunkenly together?"

"Well, suppose they should?" Raymond inquired sarcastically. "Are we to be isolationists? Don't you always spend fifty per cent of your time in New York with white people?"

"I'm glad you asked that," Dr. Parkes replied calmly. "It's not a matter of associating with white people. It's a matter of the type of white person with whom you associate."

"All right. But what was wrong with those people at the party last night? Granted they were for the most part seekers after thrills and sensation. Granted they were not paunchy philanthropists, or like Samuel here, sympathetic uplifters. Granted they were part and parcel of the lunatic fringe. But, after all, they are the people who take the lead in instituting new points of view, in exploring slightly known territory. You'll admit too that through them we meet really worthwhile people, people who can give us certain contacts we need, not necessarily because we are Negroes, but because we happen to be human beings with talent who deserve some consideration. Can't you see that my generation, or at least the more forward of my generation, is tired of being patronized and patted on the head by philanthropists and social service workers? We don't always want to have to beg and do tricks. We want to lose our racial identity as such and be acclaimed for our achievements, if any. And by achievements I do not mean the usual two penny, mediocre, undistinguished natural events which are hysterically acclaimed by your N. double A. C. P. and Urban League officials."

"I'm afraid," Dr. Parkes advanced when Raymond had finished his heated harangue, "that you have gone off on a tangent. We are concerned now only with you. I think you misjudge Samuel. He really has your welfare at heart, and so have I. We are not trying to make you lead a certain life. We are only trying to make you see that remaining in this house, as notorious as it is bound to become, as notorious as it has already become, is inimical to your development. You can't create to the best of your ability, being constantly surrounded by a group of parasites and drunken nonentities. They sap your energy. And they also give rise to public legends which will eventually include and harm you."

"I agree with you perfectly. But I insist it is my own business. My friends are my friends. They may be parasites and drunken nonentities, but they are my friends. Any protection I need from them will spring from within. And as for public legends," he shrugged his shoulders, "the public being what it is, is most welcome to any legend which may spring up around me."

"But," Samuel started to speak.

Raymond silenced him. "There is no more to say. And if you don't mind, I wish you'd excuse me. I've got to get dressed and go downtown."

Dr. Parkes and Samuel exchanged glances. They realized that their mission had failed, and that Raymond was too stubborn, too intent on following his own path, to be dissuaded by outsiders.

"Well... I must run along," Dr. Parkes said calmly. "Forgive us for breaking in on you this way after a strenuous night. It wasn't very considerate. And by the way, Ray, I have an interesting idea to take up with you write you soon"

"All right, Dr. Parkes. Good day."

"Goodbye, Ray... coming, Sam?"

"Not this minute. There's something I must say to Ray."

"All right, then. Goodbye." He quietly left the room."

"Where's Steve?" Samuel asked when Dr. Parkes had gone..

"I don't know. Now get out of here and get out damn quick.

I'm sick of you, Sam, and I hope to God you never come back here again."

"But Ray. . ."

"But Ray, hell. Confine your crusading to niggers who get lynched. I don't need it. I'm sick of you. I'm sick of all you goddamned whites, you twentieth century abolitionists. You're a bunch of puking hypocrites. And that goes for reformers of your type and the lily-livered bastards that come up here seeking thrills and pleasures."

"Then you admit. . ."

"I don't admit anything. Do you think I'm entirely a fool? Don't you think I have any sense whatsoever? Don't you think I see through all of you? Oh, get out, Sam, and for Christ's sake, leave me alone."

When Samuel had gone and the messenger boy had finally come for Stephen's clothes, Raymond suddenly decided to make an expedition to the Tombs to visit Pelham. Although he had a splitting headache, he felt that he must escape from Niggeratti Manor and from all it had come to stand for, and he also had the perverse thought that he might do penance—for what he didn't know—by making this humanitarian gesture. After all, it was rather cruel to ignore Pelham's plight altogether. Especially since he felt that he and his friends were more or less responsible for Pelham's current difficulties.

Reaching the Tombs, Raymond paced the sidewalk, circling the building four times before he could decide to enter. The grim outlines of this city prison, etched in a shadowed canyon of skyscrapers, was repulsive to view and forbidding to enter. But Raymond was bent on completing his experiment, and he entered, despite the compelling urge to return home.

Steel gates clanged shut behind him. Dour guards marked his line of progress. A register book was thrust forward for him to sign. His pockets were surreptitiously patted. There was a moment of record searching, then he was led to a huge chamber dissected by a meshed screen. On one side were the prisoners, on the other their visitors.

WALLACE THURMAN

Raymond was placed between the Irish mother of an incriminated policeman, and the Jewish sweetheart of an Italian gangster. While waiting for Pelham, he observed the other people in the room. Some were weeping, some were laughing, all were shouting through the screen, trying to be heard above the din which they were helping to create. Strange accents and unfamiliar snatches of foreign dialects imbued the room with a tower of Babel aspect. It was all so poignantly mad that Raymond wanted to fee immediately. Couples trying to kiss through the screen. Others caressing its meshed surface, striving for a feel of the flesh on the other side. An unkempt vagabond talking baby talk to a sniveling peroxide blonde. An Armenian woman clipping the air with shrill foreign expletives. A rabbi reading from a Yiddish Bible to a surly Jewish youth. A Negro in flashy clothes stage whispering and guffawing with a similarly attired Negro prisoner. Raymond's head began to reel. The scene was phantasmagorical, unreal, oppressing. The room a lethal chamber. The people flabby puppets jingling at the end of strings over which a master hand had lost control.

Raymond leaned against the screen and faced Pelham. Forcing a smile and consciously regulating the tone of his voice, informing it with an assured nonchalance, he shouted, "Hello, Pelham."

Pelham was crying. His rubicund black face was pallid, ashy. He blubbered like a baby.

"I ain't done nothin'. I ain't done nothin'," he reiterated over and over again.

Raymond was still cheery.

"We know it. Everything's going to be all right." He had to shout this through the screen four times before Pelham seemed to have heard. The Irish woman glared at Raymond and increased the volume of her own Gaelic accents. The rabbi droned on in a piercing monotone. The Negro's stage whisper and guffaws became more boisterous. The sniveling blonde blew her nose. The Jewish sweetheart blasphemed "stool pigeons." The clamor became crescendo, contrapuntal and dissonant. And from far away Pelham whined:

"I'm ruined, Ray, I'm ruined. I ain't done nothin', and they keep me in jail. An', Ray, they beat me at the station that first night, knocked me around and kicked me. An' God knows I ain't done nothin'. They'll keep me in jail forever. I'm ruined."

"Nonsense," Ray announced curtly. But the word did not carry.

"Everyone'll look down on me," Pelham continued incoherently. "I'll be a convict. My grandmother in heaven'll suffer. I'm bein' punished for not bein' a Christian like her. I'm wicked, Ray, but I ain't done nothin' an' I want a minister."

Raymond could stand no more. He felt dizzy, faint. His ears hummed with disparate echoes, jumbled, monotonous and insistent. He perspired freely as if in a sweat box. The din enveloped him, became a crushing vise, enfeebling his mind and senses. And on the other side of the screen, Pelham continued his hysterical monologue. Raymond could stand no more.

"Shut up, God damn you." He turned and hurried from the room. The guards were interminably slow in opening the gates. People and walls and steel barriers impeded his progress, but finally, he was once more in the street. The fresh air and the intermittent shafts of skyscraper-obstructed sunshine were tonic in their effect. He breathed deeply, bared his head, and walked hurriedly away. Automatic ally, he plunged into the first subway kiosk he saw, then as abruptly plunged upward into the open air. The rumble of an approaching train, the dimly lit subterranean interior, the clicking of the turnstiles and the bedlam of the crowd's cross currents were too akin to that from which he had just fled. He wanted to be in the open, to be away from constricting walls, jabbering people, and ear deafening noises. But the street afforded a poor sanctuary.

The sidewalks were crowded. Raymond walked in confused circles. He had lost all sense of direction. Excruciating pains racked his head. The conflicting currents of pedestrians pushed him first one way and then another, jostling him back and forth like an inanimate bean bag. Perspiration streamed down his face. Shrapnels of flame ricocheted from the pavement to sear his weakening body. He grew dizzy, distraught, and unexpectedly found himself leaning against a building. He felt an urge to bore into its surface and lose himself in its chilled immunity. Then the noises of the street began to recede into the distance. The people passing became inflated and floated haphazardly above the surface of the sidewalk. The buildings on the opposite side of the street leered from their multitudinous windows, and leaned precariously, a flashback to the Cabinet of Dr. Caligari.

He pressed harder and harder against the surface of the building. After what seemed hours of effort, it gave way, and his body began to penetrate into its stone. He became chilled. The buildings across the way toppled crazily downward. Let them fall. He was safe in his cranny. The protective stone had entombed him. He had achieved Nirvana, had finally found a sanctuary, finally found escape from the malevolent world which sought to destroy him. He sank back into his protective nook. The opening through which he had bored closed as if by magic and shut him out from insensate chaos. Oblivion resulted. His body slumped to the pavement, lay inert, lifeless, and was booted by the careless, rushing feet of passing pedestrians.

•••

He was on an ocean. Calm billows cradled him, transferred him gently to the shore, venting plangent roars of self-approval. Mist kissed his lips and cooled his fervid head and cheeks. Spray enveloped his naked body. Fleecy phantoms in the sky protected his eyes from the blazing sun. Then there was a gradual cessation of movement and sound. The breakers had deposited him upon something soft and yielding to the weight of his body. The phantoms had dispersed and the sun's unretarded rays blinded him. The roar of the waves diminished in volume, became pianissimo, then faded into nothingness. There was complete silence. Consciousness returned.

"How's the coon?" It was an unfamiliar male voice.

"He's coming out of it. Must be epileptic." A woman's voice penetrated the fog. Raymond opened his eyes. An immense calcimined ceiling arched above him. An acrid odor invaded his nostrils as he breathed deeply. A disembodied hand appropriated his wrist, professional fingers, cool and direct, pressed upon his pulse. His roving eyes encountered the form of a uniformed nurse bending over him. He sat up abruptly, startled. His wrist was wrenched from her restraining hand. The nurse smiled, as did the interne standing by her side.

"All right," she announced crisply and walked away. Raymond was speechless. His reconnoitering eyes discerned a hospital ward, full of beds. The interne was speaking.

"Your name Raymond Taylor?"

"Yes."

"You live at 267 West 1—th Street?"

"Yes."

"Well, we found letters in your pocket which identified you. We called your house. They'll be after you soon."

"What's the matter?" Raymond asked anxiously, unable to comprehend why he was in a hospital ward.

"You're in Bellevue. Fell out on the street. Ever do that before?"

"No."

"You're not epileptic, are you?"

"No."

"Ever have heart trouble?"

"No." Other words surged through his consciousness but could not be articulated.

"Humph." The interne turned to a table beside the bed. "Here, drink this." He forced a glass of clear liquid into Raymond's hand. Obediently the glass was drained.

"Now lie quiet a while. You can go home when someone comes after you."

He was gone. Raymond lay down and tried to re call what had happened. He seemed to have been unconscious for years. Everything was jumbled and incongruous. He fell into a stupor, and was almost asleep when Paul and Eustace, accompanied by the interne, leaned inquiringly over him.

XX

Raymond went to bed the moment he returned home from the hospital. He felt weak, depressed and ill. His head ached constantly, throbbing with all the intensity of an overworked dynamo. His nerves were taut, expectant. And yet there was really nothing wrong physically. His whole trouble was mental, and he knew it, but he did not have sufficient energy to dissipate the rather satisfying feeling of illness which enveloped him. For the moment he wanted to do nothing but lie in bed and be left alone.

Paul and Eustace respected his wishes. But Euphoria was insistent upon calling in a physician. Only by telling her that she could call one in on the next day if he felt no better was Raymond able to be rid of her.

He was lying in his bed, eyes partly closed, half awake, mind conjuring fantastic dream images, when he became aware of someone being in the room. Opening his eyes, he saw Stephen leaning over him. Stephen appeared to be ill too. The usually keen blue eyes were dull and bleary. The smooth, transparent skin was mottled, drawn, and heavily lined.

"I didn't mean to wake you."

"I wasn't asleep."

There was an awkward silence.

"Why don't you sit down? There's room on the bed."

Raymond turned over on his side so that he faced the center of the room. Stephen eased himself on to the edge of the bed, and sat there nervously twirling his hat.

"Are you surprised to see me?"

"Mmn. . . more or less."

"I heard you were ill."

"How?"

"I telephoned of course. Your messenger boy stunt hurt."

"I explained that in my note. I really didn't see any sense in our seeing one another."

"Yes. . . I know."

They fell silent again, each waiting for the other to reopen the conversation. Finally, Stephen got up, took a turn around the room, then divested himself of his hat and coat and turned to Raymond.

"Must we be so childish?" he said. "I tell you. I've got some liquor. . . some good liquor. Let's drink some and maybe our tongues will be loosened."

"But I'm ill, and I don't want to drink."

"Horse feathers. You know there isn't a damn thing wrong with you except that you're mentally drunk. Why not get physically drunk, too?"

He went into the alcove, obtained two glasses and poured out two stiff drinks. The glasses were soon empty and as quickly refilled and emptied again. After the third drink, Raymond forgot his lethargic state and sat up in the bed.

"You know, Steve," he was saying, "you ought to write the story of your experiences in Harlem and sell them to Mencken. He's so damn interested in Aframericana recently. But I doubt if he would believe it. I hardly believe it myself. I hardly believe anything that's happened in this damn house."

"This house has been bad for both of us. I often wonder what would have happened had we been in a more sane atmosphere."

"Are there any?"

"Any what?"

"Sane atmospheres. I've never found one. It seems to me that my whole life has been one whirlpool after another. I'm one of those people who are so anti-vegetable that the most insignificant event in my life takes on exciting proportions."

"Always the author, Ray, always the author. You dramatize yourself and every situation in which you find yourself. And you seem to feel that no incident which occurs around you can reach a climax unless you contribute something to the action. And the moment someone pulls something exciting, you always feel as if you must surpass them. You're as addicted to the spotlight as Paul, but you're much more subtle about it."

"Oh yeah."

"Give me your glass. Let's have another drink."

"I deserve one after that last crack." Stephen refilled the glasses. They were silent until the glasses were once more empty.

"What's going to become of you and me, Ray?"

"Who in the hell knows, and who in the hell cares! I'm going to write, probably a series of books which will cause talk but won't sell, and will be criticized severely, then forgotten. Negroes won't like nae because they'll swear I have no race pride, and white people won't like me because I won't recognize their stereotypes. Do you know, Steve, that I'm sick of both whites and blacks? I'm sick of discussing the Negro problem, of having it thrust at me from every conversational nook and cranny. I'm sick of whites who think I can't talk about anything else, and of Negroes who think I shouldn't talk about anything else. I refuse to wail and lament. My problem is a personal one, although I most certainly do not blind myself to what it means to be a Negro. I get it from all sides. I get it from the majority of whites who invade Harlem and who bend over backwards making themselves agreeable. I get it from whites downtown with whom I do business, and who for the most part are unconsciously patronizing. But I have a sense of humor. That's all that saves me from becoming like most of the Negroes I know. Things amuse me. They don't make me bitter. I may get moody and curse my fate, but so does any other human being with an ounce of intelligence. The odds are against me. .. well. . . so are they against every other man who would dare to think for himself. Most of the people who would segregate me because of my color are so inferior to me that I can only pity their ignorance, and as for those who patronize me I stand for it only because I am to be the gainer."

"What's the point?"

"I don't know. I'm just talking, Steve, because I haven't had a chance to get anything out of my system for a long time, and God knows when I'll be able to do it again. That party affected me, too, the other night. But now I can see it in a different perspective, a clearer one, I believe. Anything that will make white people and colored people come to the conclusion that after all they are all human, all committed to the serious business of living, and all with the same faults and virtues, the sooner amalgamation can take place and the Negro problem will cease to be a blot on American civilization. There'll be other blots just as bad of course, but there won't be this mass of alien people, retarding the progress of the country because they are being inculcated with complexes which can only wrack havoc. A few years ago it was the thing for all Negroes who could get an education to be professional men, doctors, lawyers, dentists, et cetera. Now, they are all trying to be artists. Negroes love to talk, love to tell the stories of their lives. They all feel that they are so different from the rest of humanity, so besieged by problems peculiar only to themselves. And since it is the fashion now to be articulate either in words, music or paint brush, every Negro, literate or otherwise, confesses and is tempted to act according to the current fad."

"How's it going to end?"

"A few Negroes will escape their race and go on about their business. In small towns throughout the country, and in some large towns too, you will find financially independent Negroes who are respected members of the community, holding responsible jobs and being taken for granted by their white neighbors. Over in Staten Island, there is a Negro who has made a fortune in the trucking business. He is a director in one of the local banks. He belongs to the chamber of commerce. And he can hardly write his name. What's the reason? He has money. He's an individualist. And that is the only type of Negro who will ever escape from the shroud of color, those who go on about their own business, and do what they can in the best way they can, whether it be in business or in art. Eventually only the Babbitt and the artist will be able to break the chains. The rest must wait until the inevitable day of complete assimilation."

"Won't the masses benefit by Communism if they are given the chance?"

"I'm glad you spoke of that, for I, for one, would like to see them get the chance. I'd like to help disseminate communistic propaganda among the black masses. Just to see if their resentment is near enough the surface to be inflamed. I'd like to see them retaliate against the whites in their own sphere. For every lynching, I'd like to see Negroes take their toll in whites. If I thought that the Negro masses would be belligerent enough to fight for their rights, and make capitalistic America stop playing black labor against white labor, I'd join the communist party tomorrow and risk life and limb spreading the gospel."

"You're contradicting yourself. How can you fight both for the masses and for the individual? I've heard you say a million times that there is nothing to be looked for from the proletarian Negro. That only the individual matters. And that you would waste more energy protesting against the false imprisonment of a Mooney and a Billings than you would against the lynching of some stray darky who probably deserved no better fate."

"Right you are, Steve. But after all, you have to improve the status of the masses in order to develop your individuals. It is mass movements which bring forth individuals. I don't care about stray darkies getting lynched, but I do care about people who will fight for a principle. And if out of a wholesale allegiance to Communism, the Negro could develop just a half dozen men who were really and truly outstanding, the result would be worth the effort. I'm sick of the namby-pamby folk who call themselves leaders of the race. Booker T. was a great man. Frederick Douglass was a great man. Garvey was a great man with obvious limitations. He was an organizer, which is something no other Negro leader can boast of being. As a race leader, DuBois is a potentially great writer gone wrong, and the rest are mere chicken feed, pushed into prominence because of expediency." Raymond paused and drew a deep breath. "Now, for God's sake, give me a drink."

Stephen complied with his request. And after Raymond had drained his glass, he suddenly turned to Stephen:

"Jeez. I've been raving like an idiot for the last hour. You asked me what was going to become of you and me. I haven't answered either, have I? Well, what is going to happen to you?"

"Let's don't talk about me. I'm not important. I can never be anything but a camp follower. I'll never have the courage to rush in front of any vanguard. I'll probably spend all my time on the wide public highway, avoiding any unchartered side path. You see, I'm one of Gertrude Stein's lost generation. . . or rather post-lost generation. I'm too busy trying to find borderlines in this new universe of ours ever to strike out on my own. I'm afraid of the dark, I sup pose. The world has become too large. I can't see the skyline from the ground, and I'll probably become a Humanist just because they are interested in establishing boundary lines."

"Why not revolt?"

"There's really very little to revolt against since the Victorians have been so thoroughly demolished. And it's too soon to rebel against the present régime of demolition. Of course the real reason is that I am too easily seduced by the semblance of security to risk the loss of creature comfort."

"In that case you don't deserve any sympathy."

"Sez you with an air of superiority. For all your prattle about self-sufficiency, egoism, revolt, individuality, and sense of humor, your flight, too, will be curtailed, and you, like myself, will be pressed downwards, and forced to cry out with Santayana:

'I would I might forget that I am I

And break the heavy chain that binds me fast,

Whose links about myself my deeds have cast.'"

Stephen paused for a moment. "Maybe I'm wrong. You have something to fight for and against. You've got to fight two sets of people, your own and mine. . . "

"And get a hearing from neither. No, Steve, I wish that I could lead a vegetable existence. It sounds romantic, but

I suppose I'm bound to thrive on antagonism. I'd be bored to death otherwise. I'll probably spend my life doing things just to make people angry. I don't expect to be a great writer. I don't think the Negro race can produce one now, any more than can America. I know of only one Negro who has the elements of greatness, and that's Jean Toomer. The rest of us are merely journeymen, planting seed for someone else to harvest. We all get sidetracked sooner or later. The older ones become warped by propaganda. We younger ones are mired in decadence. None of us seem able to rise above our environment. That donation party the other night is symptomatic of my generation. We're a curiosity. . . even to ourselves. It will be some years before the more forward will be accepted as human beings and allowed to associate with giants. The pygmies have taken us over now, and I doubt if any of us has the strength to use them for a stepladder to a higher plane."

"What's the solution?"

"I should know!"

"But what are you going to do?"

"Eventually I'm going to renounce Harlem and all it stands for now. You see, Harlem has become a state of mind, peopled with improbable monsters. There are a quarter million Negroes here, and it is fashionable only to take notice of a bare thousand the cabaret entertainers, the actors, the musicians, the artists, and the colorful minority who drift from rent party to speakeasy to side-street dives. The rest are ignored. They're not interesting. Because we live in an age when only the abnormal is interesting."

"You're wrong there, Ray. The abnormal is receding into its proper sphere."

"Oh yeah? That accounts, I suppose, for the popularity of Faulkner and Hemingway. They are so interested in normality. No, Steve, there is not yet a return to normalcy, and certainly not for the Negro who has never known such a state. He is, you see, a product of his age and of his race, which has been carried along at such a pace that never has there been time

WALLACE THURMAN

for him to sit by the side of the road and reflect upon what it all might mean."

Stephen refilled their glasses. Both were tired now. Silently they made a gesture of toasting one another, then downed their drinks. Stephen placed now. the empty glasses and the empty flask upon the table, and in doing this, noticed a notebook, dirty, dogeared, and worn, carelessly thrown atop a pile of books.

"What's this?" he asked, picking it up.

"Oh, that's Paul's notebook. Bring it here. There's something in it I must show you."

Stephen handed the notebook to Raymond, who busied himself turning the grimy pages. He finally found the page he sought, and, smiling, handed the notebook to Stephen.

"Get a load of this, will ya?"

Dear Gabriele D'Annunzio (Stephen read):

Susceptible as you are to flattery (for all great men are vain)

I do not follow in the footsteps of the herd. For I, too, am an artist. A genius. I, too, have visions. And you interest me. Spectacular person. Your cleverness amuses me. Witty man. Your idiosyncrasies intrigue me. Wise One. I am only delayed in making you a visit by financial difficulty. But that is a minor hindrance and one that you may alleviate to save yourself further expectancy. For I am coming. Expect me.

Paul Arbian

P.S. Your cell of pure dreams is wonderful in conception. But faulty in a few details. I know you better than you know yourself.

"What the hell?" Stephen began.

"Turn to the next page," Raymond said. "You ain't seen nothing yet." Stephen turned the page and read:

The Shah of Persia:
Illustrious potentates need jewels to enhance their own immortal luster.

You lack the most priceless jewel best to set yourself off. I am that jewel. An artist. A genius. A citizen of the world. You could array me in a setting befitting my personality. And you can send me the fare enabling me to come to you. I'll be the correct something you need to make your exile in Paris a thing of joy and beauty forever.

I await your answer. Ignoring me will not appreciably delay my coming. It is written. . .

Paul Arbian

"But," Stephen was completely bewildered, "is this a part of his novel?"

"That's what I thought when I first saw them. But Paul informed me, very haughtily I assure you, that they were copies of letters he had mailed over a month ago. I was too dumbfounded to speak."

"But. . . the audacity. He must be crazy."

"Not crazy, Steve. . . merely an illustration of my statement that the more intellectual and talented Negroes of my generation are among the most pathetic people in the world today."

XXI

After Stephen's unexpected visit and their long conversation together, Raymond seemed to have developed a new store of energy. For three days and nights, he had secluded himself in his room, and devoted all his time to the continuance of his novel. For three years it had remained a project. Now he was making rapid progress. The ease with which he could work once he set himself to it amazed him, and at the same time he was suspicious of this unexpected facility. Nevertheless, his novel was progressing, and he intended to let nothing check him.

In line with this resolution, he insisted that Paul and Eustace hold their nightly gin parties without his presence, and they were also abjured to steer all company clear of his studio.

Stephen had gone upstate on a tutoring job.

Lucille had not been in evidence since the donation party, and Raymond had made no attempt to get in touch with her. There was no one else in whom he had any interest. Aline and Janet he had dismissed from his mind, although Eustace and Paul had spent an entire dinner hour telling him of their latest adventures. Both had now left Aline's mother's house and were being supported by some white man, whom Aline had met at a downtown motion picture theater. They had an apartment in which they entertained groups of young colored boys on the nights their white protector was not in evidence.

Having withdrawn from every activity connected with Niggeratti Manor, Raymond had also forgotten that Dr. Parkes had promised to communicate with him, concerning some mysterious idea, and he was taken by surprise when Eustace came into the room one morning, bearing a letter from Dr. Parkes.

"Well, I'm plucked," Raymond exclaimed. "What's the matter?" Eustace queried.

"Will you listen to this?" He read the letter aloud.

"My dear Raymond:

I will be in New York on Thursday night. I want you to do me a favor. It seems to me that with the ever increasing number of younger Negro artists and intellectuals gathering in Harlem, some effort should be made to establish what well might become a distinguished salon. All of you engaged in creative work, should, I believe, welcome the chance to meet together once every fortnight, for the purpose of exchanging ideas and expressing and criticizing in dividual theories. This might prove to be both stimulating and profitable. And it might also bring into active being a concerted movement which would establish the younger Negro talent once and for all as a vital artistic force. With this in mind, I would appreciate your inviting as many of your colleagues as possible to your studio on Thursday evening. I will be there to preside. I hope you are intrigued by the idea and willing to cooperate. Please wire me your answer. Collect, of course.
Very sincerely yours,

Dr. A. L. Parkes."

"Are you any more good?" Raymond asked as he finished reading.

"Sounds like a great idea," Eustace replied enthusiastically.

"It *is* great. Too great to miss," Raymond acquiesced mischievously. "Come on, let's get busy on the telephone."

• • •

Thursday night came and so did the young hopefuls. The first to arrive was Sweetie May Carr. Sweetie May was a

WALLACE THURMAN

short story writer, more noted for her ribald wit and personal effervescence than for any actual literary work. She was a great favorite among those whites who went in for Negro prodigies. Mainly because she lived up to their conception of what a typical Negro should be. It seldom occurred to any of her patrons that she did this with tongue in cheek. Given a paleface audience, Sweetie May would launch forth into a saga of the little all-colored Mississippi town where she claimed to have been born. Her repertoire of tales was earthy, vulgar and funny. Her darkies always smiled through their tears, sang spirituals on the slightest provocation, and performed buck dances when they should have been working. Sweetie May was a master of southern dialect, and an able raconteur, but she was too indifferent to literary creation to transfer to paper that which she told so well. The intricacies of writing bored her, and her written work was for the most part turgid and unpolished. But Sweetie May knew her white folks.

"It's like this," she had told Raymond. "I have to eat. I also wish to finish my education. Being a Negro writer these days is a racket and I'm going to make the most of it while it lasts. Sure I cut the fool. But I enjoy it, too. I don't know a tinker's damn about art. I care less about it. My ultimate ambition, as you know, is to become a gynecologist. And the only way I can live easily until I have the requisite training is to pose as a writer of potential ability, *voila*! I get my tuition paid at Columbia. I rent an apartment and have all the furniture contributed by kindhearted o'fays. I receive bundles of groceries from various sources several times a week. . . all accomplished by dropping a discreet hint during an evening's festivities. I find queer places for whites to go in Harlem. . . out of the way primitive churches, side street speakeasies. They fall for it. About twice a year I manage to sell a story. It is acclaimed. I am a genius in the making. Thank God for this Negro literary renaissance! Long may it flourish!"

Sweetie May was accompanied by two young girls, recently emigrated from Boston. They were the latest to be hailed as incipient immortals. Their names were Doris Westmore and Hazel Jamison. Doris wrote short stories. Hazel wrote poetry. Both had become known through a literary contest fostered by one of the leading Negro magazines. Raymond liked them more than he did most of the younger recruits to the movement. For one thing, they were characterized by a freshness and naïveté which he and his cronies had lost. And, surprisingly enough for Negro prodigies, they actually gave promise of possessing literary talent. He was most pleased to see them. He was also amused by their interest and excitement. A salon! A literary gathering! It was one of the civilized institutions they had dreamed of finding in New York, one of the things they had longed and hoped for.

As time passed, others came in. Tony Crews, smiling and self-effacing, a mischievous boy, grateful for the chance to slip away from the backwoods college he attended. Raymond had never been able to analyze this young poet. His work was interesting and unusual. It was also spotty. Spasmodically he gave promise of developing into a first rate poet. Already he had published two volumes, prematurely, Raymond thought. Both had been excessively praised by whites and universally damned by Negroes. Considering the nature of his work this was to be expected. The only unknown quantity was the poet himself. Would he or would he not fulfill the promise exemplified in some of his work? Raymond had no way of knowing and even an intimate friendship with Tony himself had failed to enlighten him. For Tony was the most close-mouthed and cagey individual Raymond had ever known when it came to personal matters. He fended off every attempt to probe into his inner self and did this with such an unconscious and naïve air that the prober soon came to one of two conclusions: Either Tony had no depth whatsoever, or else he was too deep for plumbing by ordinary mortals.

DeWitt Clinton, the Negro poet laureate, was there, too, accompanied, as usual, by his *fideles achates*, David Holloway. David had been ac claimed the most handsome Negro in Harlem by a certain group of whites. He was in great demand by artists who wished to paint him. He had become a much touted romantic figure. In reality he was a fairly intelligent schoolteacher, quite circumspect in his habits, a rather timid beau, who imagined himself to be bored with life.

Dr. Parkes finally arrived, accompanied by Carl Denny, the artist, and Carl's wife, Annette. Next to arrive was Cedric Williams, a West Indian, whose first book, a collection of short stories with a Caribbean background, in Raymond's opinion, marked him as one of the three Negroes writing who actually had something to say, and also some concrete idea of style. Cedric was followed by Austin Brown, a portrait painter whom Raymond personally despised, a Dr. Manfred Trout, who practiced medicine and also wrote exceptionally good short stories, Glenn Madison, who was a Communist, and a long, lean professorial person, Allen Fenderson, who taught school and had ambitions to become a crusader modeled after W. E. B. Du Bois.

The roster was now complete. There was an hour of small talk and drinking of mild cocktails in order to induce case and allow the various guests to become acquainted and voluble. Finally, Dr. Parkes ensconced himself in Raymond's favorite chair, where he could get a good view of all in the room, and clucked for order.

Raymond observed the professor closely. Paul's description never seemed more apt. He was a mother ben clucking at her chicks. Small, dapper, with sensitive features, graying hair, a dominating head, and restless hands and feet, he smiled benevolently at his brood. Then, in his best continental manner, which be had acquired during four years at European Universities, he began to speak.

"You are," he perorated, "the outstanding personalities in a new generation. On you depends the future of your race. You are not, as were your predecessors, concerned with donning armor, and clashing swords with the enemy in the public square. You are finding both an escape and a weapon in beauty, which beauty when created by you will cause the American white man to reestimate the Negro's value to his civilization, cause him to realize that the American black man is too valuable, too potential of utilitarian accomplishment, to be kept downtrodden and segregated.

"Because of your concerted storming up Parnassus, new vistas will be spread open to the entire race. The Negro in the south will no more know peonage, Jim Crowism, or loss of the ballot, and the Negro everywhere in America will know complete freedom and equality.

"But," and here his voice took on a more serious tone, "to accomplish this, your pursuit of beauty must be vital and lasting. I am somewhat fearful of the decadent strain which seems to have filtered into most of your work. Oh, yes, I know you are children of the age and all that, but you must not, like your paleface contemporaries, wallow in the mire of post-Victorian license. You have too much at stake. You must have ideals. You should become. . . well, let me suggest your going back to your racial roots, and cultivating a healthy paganism based on African traditions.

"For the moment that is all I wish to say. I now want you all to give expression to your own ideas. Perhaps we can reach a happy mean for guidance."

He cleared his throat and leaned contentedly back in his chair. No one said a word. Raymond was full of contradictions, which threatened to ooze forth despite his efforts to remain silent. But he knew that once the ooze began there would be no stop ping the flood, and he was anxious to hear what some of the others might have to say.

However, a glance at the rest of the people in the nom assured him that most of them had not the slightest understanding of what had been said, nor any ideas on the subject, whatsoever. Once more Dr. Parkes clucked for discussion. No one ventured a word. Raymond could see that Cedric, like himself, was full of argument, and also like him, did not wish to appear contentious at such an early stage in the discussion. Tony winked at Raymond when be caught his eye, but the expression on his face was as inscrutable as ever. Sweetie May giggled behind her handkerchief. Paul amused himself by sketching the various people in the room. The rest were blank.

"Come, come, now," Dr. Parkes urged somewhat impatiently, "I'm not to do all the talking. What have you to say, DeWitt?"

All eyes sought out the so-called Negro poet laureate. For a moment he stirred uncomfortably in his chair, then in a high pitched, nasal voice proceeded to speak.

"I think, Dr. Parkes, that you have said all there is to say, I agree with you. The young Negro artist must go back to his pagan heritage for inspiration. and to the old masters for form."

Raymond could not suppress a snort. For De Witt's few words had given him a vivid mental picture of that poet's creative hours—eyes on a page of Keats, fingers on typewriter, mind frantic ally conjuring African scenes. And there would of course be a Bible nearby.

Paul had ceased being intent on his drawing long enough to hear "pagan heritage," and when DeWitt finished he inquired inelegantly:

"What old black pagan heritage?"

DeWitt gasped, surprised and incredulous.

"Why, from your ancestors."

"Which ones?" Paul pursued dumbly.

"Your African ones, of course." DeWitt's voice was full of disdain.

"What about the rest?"

"What rest?" He was irritated now.

"My German, English and Indian ancestors," Paul answered willingly. "How can I go back to African ancestors when their blood is so diluted and their country and times so far away? I have no conscious affinity for them at all."

Dr. Parkes intervened: "I think you've missed the point, Paul."

"And I," Raymond was surprised at the sudden ness with which he joined in the argument, "think he has hit the nail right on the head. Is there really any reason why *all* Negro artists should consciously and deliberately dig into African soil for inspiration and material unless they actually wish to do so?"

"I don't mean that. I mean you should develop your inherited spirit."

DeWitt beamed. The doctor had expressed his own hazy theory. Raymond was about to speak again, when Paul once more took the bit between his own teeth.

"I ain't got no African spirit."

Sweetie May giggled openly at this, as did Carl Denny's wife, Annette. The rest looked appropriately sober, save for Tony, whose eyes continued to telegraph mischievously to Raymond. Dr. Parkes tried to squelch Paul with a frown. He should have known better.

"I'm not an African," the culprit continued. "I'm an American and a perfect product of the melting pot,"

"That's nothing to brag about." Cedric spoke for the first time.

"And I think you're all on the wrong track." All eyes were turned toward this new speaker, Allen Fenderson. "Dr. Du Bois has shown us the way. We must be militant fighters. We must not hide away in ivory towers and prate of beauty. We must fashion cudgels and bludgeons rather than sensitive plants. We must excoriate the white man, and make him grant us justice. We must fight for complete social and political and economic equality."

"What we ought to do," Glenn Madison growled intensely, "is to join hands with the workers of the world and overthrow the present capitalistic régime. We are of the proletariat and must fight our battles allied with them, rather than singly and selfishly."

"All of us?" Raymond inquired quietly.

"All of us who have a trace of manhood and are more interested in the rights of human beings than in gin parties and neurotic capitalists."

"I hope you're squelched," Paul stage whispered to Raymond.

"And how!" Raymond laughed. Several joined in. Dr. Parkes spoke quickly to Fenderson, ignoring the remarks of the Communist.

"But, Fenderson this is a new generation and must make use of new weapons. Some of us will continue to fight in the old way, but there are other things to be considered, too. Remember, a beautiful sonnet can be as effectual, nay even more effectual, than a rigorous hymn of hate."

"The man who would understand and be moved by a hymn of hate would not bother to read your sannet and, even if he did, he would not know what it was all about."

"I don't agree. Your progress must be a boring in from the top, not a battle from the bottom. Convert the higher beings and the lower orders will automatically follow."

"Spoken like a true capitalistic minion," Glenn Madison muttered angrily.

Fenderson prepared to continue his argument, but he was forestalled by Cedric.

"What does it matter," he inquired diffidently, "what any of you do so long as you remain true to yourselves? There is no necessity for this movement becoming standardized. There is ample room for everyone to follow his own individual track. Dr. Parkes wants us all to go back to Africa and resurrect our pagan heritage, become atavistic. In this he is supported by Mr. Clinton. Fenderson here wants us all to be propagandists and yell at the top of our lungs at every conceivable injustice. Madison wants us all to take a cue from Leninism and fight the capitalistic bogey. Well. . . why not let each young hopeful choose his own path? Only in that way will anything at all be achieved."

"Which is just what I say," Raymond smiled gratefully at Cedric. "One cannot make movements. nor can one plot their course. When the work of a given number of individuals during a given period is looked at in retrospect, then one can identify a movement and evaluate its distinguishing characteristics. Individuality is what we should strive for. Let each seek his own salvation. To me, a wholesale flight back to Africa or a wholesale allegiance to Communism or a wholesale adherence to an antiquated and for the most part ridiculous propagandistic program are all equally futile and unintelligent."

Dr. Parkes gasped and sought for an answer. Cedric forestalled him.

"To talk of an African heritage among American Negroes is unintelligent. It is only in the West Indies that you can find direct descendants from African ancestors. Your primitive instincts among all but the extreme proletariat have been ironed out. You're standardized Americans."

"Oh, no," Carl Denny interrupted suddenly. "You're wrong. It's in our blood. It's. . . " he fumbled for a word, "fixed. Why. . . " he stammered again, "remember Cullen's poem, *Heritage*:

> *'So I lie who find no peace*
> *Night or day, no slight release*
> *From the unremittent beat*
> *Made by cruel padded feet.*
> *Walking through my body's street.*
> *Up and down they go, and back,*
> *Treading out a jungle track.'*

"We're all like that. Negroes are the only people in America not standardized. The feel of the African jungle is in their blood. Its rhythms surge through their bodies. Look how Negroes laugh and dance and sing, all spontaneous and individual."

"Exactly," Dr. Parkes and DeWitt nodded assent.

"I have yet to see an intelligent or middle class American Negro laugh and sing and dance spontaneously. That's an illusion, a pretty sentimental fiction. Moreover your songs and dances are not in dividual. Your spirituals are mediocre folk songs, ignorantly culled from Methodist hymn books. There are white men who can sing them just as well as Negroes, if not better, should they happen to be untrained vocalists like Robeson, rather than highly trained technicians like Hayes. And as for dancing spontaneously and feeling the rhythms of the jungle... humph!"

Sweetie May jumped into the breach.

"I can do the Charleston better than any white person."

"I particularly stressed... intelligent people.

The lower orders of any race have more vim and vitality than the illuminated tenth."

Sweetie May leaped to her feet.

"Why, you West Indian... "

"Sweetie, Sweetie," Dr. Parkes was shocked by her polysyllabic expletive.

Pandemonium reigned. The master of ceremonies could not cope with the situation. Cedric called Sweetie an illiterate southern hussy. She called him all types of profane West Indian monkey chasers. DeWitt and David were shocked and showed it. The literary doctor, the Communist and Fenderson moved uneasily around the room. Annette and Paul Filed. The two child prodigies from Boston looked wide-eyed, utterly bewildered and dismayed. Raymond leaned back in his chair, puffing on a cigarette, detached and amused. Austin, the portrait painter, audibly repeated over and over to himself: "Just like niggers.. just like niggers." Carl Denny interposed himself between Cedric and Sweetie May. Dr. Parkes clucked for civilized behavior, which came only when Cedric stalked angrily out of the room.

After the alien had been routed and peace restored, Raymond passed a soothing cocktail. Meanwhile Austin and Carl had begun arguing about painting. Carl did not possess a facile tongue. He always had difficulty formulating in words the multitude of ideas which seethed in his mind. Austin, to quote Raymond, was an illiterate cad. Having examined one of Carl's pictures on Raymond's wall, he had disparaged it. Raymond listened attentively to their argument. He despised Austin mainly because he spent most of his time imploring noted white people to give him a break by posing for a portrait. Having the gift of making himself pitiable, and having a glib tongue when it came to expatiating in the trials and tribulations of being a Negro, he found many sitters, all of whom thought they were encouraging a handicapped Negro genius. After one glimpse at the completed portrait, they invariably changed their minds.

"I tell you," he shouted, "your pictures are distorted and grotesque. Art is art, I say. And art holds a mirror up to nature. No mirror would reflect a man composed of angles. God did not make man that way. Look at Sargent's portraits. He was an artist."

"But he wasn't," Carl expostulated. "We. . . we of this age. We must look at Matisse, Gauguin, Picasso and Renoir for guidance. They get the feel of the age. . . they. . . "

"Are all crazy and so are you," Austin countered before Carl could proceed.

Paul rushed to Carl's rescue. He quoted Wilde in rebuttal: Nature imitates art, then went on to blaspheme Sargent. Carl, having found some words to express a new idea fermenting in his brain, forgot the argument at hand, went off on a tangent and began telling the dazed Dr. Parkes about the Negroid quality in his drawings. DeWitt yawned and consulted his watch. Raymond mused that he probably resented having missed the prayer meeting which he attended every Thursday night. In another corner of the room the Communist and Fenderson had locked horns over the ultimate solution of the Negro problem. In loud voices each contended for his own particular solution. Karl Marx and Lenin were pitted against Du Bois and his disciples. The writing doctor, bored to death, slipped quietly from the room without announcing his departure or even saying goodnight. Being more intelligent than most of the others, he had wisely kept silent. Tony and Sweetie May had taken adjoining chairs, and were soon engaged in comparing their versions of original verses to the St. James Infirmary, which Tony con tended was soon to become as epical as the St. Louis Blues, Annette and Howard began gossiping about various outside personalities. The child prodigies looked from one to the other, silent, perplexed, uncomfortable, not knowing what to

WALLACE THURMAN

do or say. Dr. Parkes visibly recoiled from Carl's incoherent expository barrage, and wilted in his chair, willing but unable to effect a courteous exit. Raymond sauntered around the room, dispensing cocktails, chuck ling to himself.

Such was the first and last salon.

XXII

Raymond had been to Pelham's trial and it had left a decidedly bad taste in his mouth. The machinery of justice was a depressing contraption, and the spectacle of the moronic Pelham help less in its impersonal maw was certainly not an edifying performance. According to the laws of the state, Pelham most certainly deserved the penalty which had been meted out to him, although the indeterminate sentence of from one to three years seemed excessive. But that is what the statute books decreed for an adult who was found guilty of being sexually intimate with a minor under the age of consent. And Pelham had been found guilty.

On the witness stand he had tearfully admitted to such a misdemeanor. It was by no means a case of rape. The girl, despite her youth, was no virgin. She had known what she was about. She had even admitted, under pressure, similar experiences with at least three youngsters with whom she had gone to school.

On the other hand, Pelham had testified that he had remained chaste until his experiences with Gladys. He had, it seemed, never kept company with any girl. While his grandmother lived, he had been kept too busy waiting on her white folk to form outside contacts. And until he had moved into Niggeratti Manor, he had never before met any women who might, perchance have willing dispositions.

Raymond remembered now with a tinge of regret how he and Paul had once questioned Pelham about his sex life, and twitted him unmercifully when he had declared himself to be an uninitiate.

"You are repressed," they had cried. "A man of your age with no sexual experience is liable to develop all sorts of neuroses and complexes. You're inhibited and should let yourself go." He had let himself go. And, as a result of their advice, had become, in the unintelligent eyes of the law and the public at large, a vile creature deserving little

WALLACE THURMAN

con sideration. A sad denouement for so helpless and naïve a creature, a sad interlude in the life of one who had been seduced by the elusive spectre of future artistic success. He was now a convict, and in Pelham's simple mind, nothing could be more disastrous and degrading.

So the trial had left a bad taste in Raymond's mouth. Courts of Justice were such sadistic organizations. They seemed to gloat and thrive over the writhings of their victims. The more meager the offense, the more simple the individual, the less pity and leniency he merited. Pelham had been branded a moral leper. The seductive and knowing girl had been whitewashed as a adolescent.

And yet the trial had had its amusing moments. There had been for instance the girl's mother, who, being histrionically inclined, had striven to play the star role throughout the depressing proceedings. She had cried for justice. Her cheeild had been in a state of innocence until she had been tutored by this lecherous monster, adverse testimony to the contrary notwithstanding. The mother was a lone woman, deserted by an unworthy husband, left alone to steer two young girls through the dangerous period of adolescent life. Surely the law would not leave her and her kind exposed to such perils as Pelham personified. Surely the judge, in his mercy, could do naught but severely punish this menace to young girls. And being sympathetic and merciful, the judge had done his bit to the full extent of the law.

The surprise of the day had come when the Pig Woman had appeared as the chief witness for the prosecution. Raymond had practically forgotten her existence, and on hearing her called to the witness stand, and noting the malicious glee with which she hurried forward to testify, had immediately opined that Pelham would not escape punishment.

Her testimony had been decisive and damning. In an exultant whiny voice, she had eagerly told, how, peering through a crack in her door, she had seen Pelham chasing Gladys up and down stairs and around the hallways "with no good look in his eye," drawing her lustfully into his arms, and showering her lips with passionate kisses. Ah, yes, she had known what he had been about. She had made it her business to keep tab of every inning in his vile game. She had even made notations of the dates and hours which marked his unholy and lustful quest. She did not explain why she had not informed the girl's mother.

Raymond had never considered the Pig Woman positively before. Ofttimes he and his friends had made fun of her and speculated fantastically about her life, but at no time had they considered her as being anything more than a harmless old woman. But now, it seemed, she was an instrument of God, and she praised His Holy Name for punishing one of a group of sinners. Perhaps now the others would realize the extent of His power and change their sinful way of living before it was too late. Pelham's downfall was to be taken as a warning to his equally sinful friends, who defiled the house in which she had quietly lived for so long a time.

And thus it went. The Pig Woman was an instrument of God. The actress lady was the personification of martyred motherhood. The allegedly defiled girl was the symbol of injured chastity. The judge was a merciful instrument of justice. And Pelham was a communal menace, for whom three years in jail was not sufficient punishment for his crime against society.

Euphoria was still optimistic, however. Having failed to effect Pelham's release before imprisonment, she was now going to concentrate on having him paroled at the earliest possible moment. "A little coin. A little coin," she had said, "a few words with certain undercover men I know and Pelham will serve only a scant portion of his term." Raymond rather admired her materialistic confidence.

Lucille had arranged to have dinner with Raymond on the day of the trial. She was anxious to know its outcome, and she had also told Raymond over the telephone that she must have a talk with him. There was something most important which she must tell him. She could give him no hint of its nature until they were face to face, but it was most urgent and

WALLACE THURMAN

necessary that she see him at the earliest possible moment. Being engrossed in the trial and with his reactions to it, he had not speculated about the mysterious matter. In fact he had completely forgotten it by the time he and Lucille met in Tabbs for dinner. He told her about the trial.

"It's too bad he got the works, but there's nothing to be done, is there?"

"No, I suppose not. It seems a pity. Why didn't they lock Paul and me up, too? We are as guilty as he. And as for the girl, she deserves much more punishment than Pelham."

"What are they going to do with her?"

"Parole her in the custody of her mother so that she can continue her schooling."

"It is a mess, but we might as well forget it, and anyway I have something else more important to talk about."

"Yeah? What is it?"

"I told you over the 'phone I had something to tell you."

"That's right. I had forgotten. What is it?"

"I'm pregnant."

Raymond's eyes bulged. His mouth opened. His water glass was overturned. A waiter rushed over to repair the damage. When he had gone Raymond recovered his power of speech.

"You're pregnant!"

"Yes, and you needn't shout it all over the place."

Her coolness amazed him. It also served to reduce his own temperature.

"Bull, I suppose," he finally growled.

"Yes."

"Well... does he know it?"

"Certainly. I told him last night. He went into a rage. Accused me first of ignorance, then of conniving to get a husband, socked me in the jaw, and stalked away."

"Are you being serious?"

"I assure you it's no joking matter."

"Well, what am I supposed to do? Give my name to Bull's child?"

"It won't be necessary for it to have a name." Her calmness angered him.

"Then what the hell is this confab about?"

"Just this. I want you to help me find a doctor."

"A doctor? For what?"

To perform an abortion."

"Well, I'll be damned."

"Rather simple request, no?"

"Too damn simple. I sincerely hope that you—" he stopped short.

"That I what?"

"Have your fill of virile men. I wasn't good enough for you, was I? Around me you were always the frigid woman whom I had to keep distance from, and now." he finished weakly, unable to give expression to the emotional anger which surged within him, "look at you."

"Don't be so melodramatic, Ray. I thought you hated scenes. This is the time for you to utilize your much vaunted reason. The brain must rule, you, know, or at least that is what you always say. I'm making a very simple request. And I know that I can depend on you to help me." Then as her companion said nothing, she added, "Let's eschew dessert and hasten to a speakeasy. I have already composed a toast in honor of my abortion. I'm sure you'll appreciate it. Come on, let's barge."

She signaled to the waiter, asked for the check, slipped Raymond the necessary money, and led the way out into the street.

• • •

For the next few days, Raymond and Lucille spent most of their time obtaining information about physicians who specialized in illegal operations. Discreet inquiries netted them many addresses. There seemed to be no dearth of competent specialists. The only problem was to find one who would do the job cheaply.

From place to place they tramped, following every clue, seeking for a bargain like astute budget followers. The most expensive place was a luxurious establishment on Vanderbilt Avenue, near the Grand Central Station. The location foretold the prohibitive fee, but the two adventurers visited the place anyway, as a matter of record.

They entered the reception room of a large and sumptuously furnished suite of offices. A uniformed nurse greeted them pleasantly and escorted them into a cheerily furnished anteroom. Within a few moments they were confronted by a dignified, soft voiced physician. Raymond was the spokesman. They were, he perorated—adhering to a previously rehearsed procedure—a free love pair, both engaged in creative work. A baby at this time would be decidedly unwelcome and an economic disaster. The doctor was business like and matter of fact. Raymond liked his terse explanation of method. He oozed efficiency. But his price was two hundred and fifty dollars.

Their list was practically exhausted when they finally found a physician who charged only fifty dollars. And they had about decided on him when Euphoria came forward with the information that she knew an Italian midwife in Greenwich Village who would do the job for twenty-five. There was no more hesitation. Raymond faded into the background. Euphoria, as was her wont, took the matter into her own hands. Lucille was introduced to the lady, arrangements were completed, and in almost no time, and with little ill-effect, her body had been rid of Bull's seed once and for all.

"Well, old dear, I'm a free woman."

"Permanently, I hope?"

"The gods willing." They both laughed.

"And no more virile men?"

"At least not for the purpose of procreation. I never want to bring a child into this world. I agree with you, although I doubt your sincerity, that race suicide would be the quickest way to cure human beings of their ills. Why should we go on bringing others into the world?"

"For no reason at all, as far as I can see. It would be a grand day when the entire human race would be rendered sterile... a grand joke on the cantankerous old creator of our universe. I would chuckle with glee if one by one the inhabitants of this foolish old world would drop dead with no newly born replicas to don their shoes. That, in my opinion, is true anarchism."

"Please don't get philosophical. Is there anything to ink here?"

"Nary a drop."

"Where's Eustace and Paul?"

"Eustace has gone downtown for his audition. God alone knows where Paul is."

"Is he still doing nothing?"

"Always has, always will. I'm afraid it's his destiny."

"Has he had any new adventures recently?"

"Paul always has adventures. He can't walk down the street without returning to tell us about some thrilling new experience. It's too bad his real world is not as romantic as the world of his imagination. I envy him that, though."

"No you don't, Ray, for some day he is going to face reality and the shock perhaps will be too great for him to weather."

"Perhaps so... but... " moment... he hesitated a moment...

"Don't you hear music?"

"I thought so. Perhaps Eustace is back. Let's go down and see how he came out."

"O. K."

They left the room and descended the stairs. Raymond was startled by the discordant banging which assailed their ears.

"What could be wrong? Eustace never bangs a piano like that."

As they reached the door leading to his room, the aimless banging ceased. They hesitated before knocking. Listening, they heard the sound of tearing paper. Eustace seemed to be in a frenzy. Hurriedly Raymond opened the door. He and Lucille entered. Their presence was unnoted. Attired in his green dressing gown, Eustace was frantically destroying every sheet of music atop his piano.

"What on earth is the matter?"

He turned on them angrily. His seamed face was more drawn than ever. Tears streamed down the wrinkles, forming little rivulets. His hair was awry, exposing his usually hidden bald spot.

"Get out. Get out and take your spirituals with you. Get out, I say." There was a flurry of torn paper.

"But Eustace…"

"Get out. Don't you hear? Spirituals, spirituals, yeah, I'll sing spirituals."

"But what happened?" Raymond was certain he knew the answer to his question.

"I hope you're all happy. You urged me to sing spirituals. It was the only way I could gain a hearing. Well, I sang them and they. . . " his voice broke into a sob, "they said I wasn't good enough. That competition was too great. . . and I. . . didn't get a chance to sing Schubert."

He dropped to the piano bench. His head and arms slumped to the keys. A jumbled melange of discords drowned out his sobs.

XXIII

W̶ell, Ray, how's every little thing?"

"Pretty fair, Aline. Where've you been so long?"

"Where've I been? I've been here almost every night. You wouldn't see me."

"I've been busy. Where's Janet?"

"I don't know. We're not friends anymore."

"Not friends?" Raymond exclaimed. "Well, that *is* news. What caused the grand bustup this time?"

"Jealousy."

"Still fighting over some man?"

"Not exactly. You see, Ray. . . I'm gonna pass for white."

"What man inspired this?"

"Oh, he's a swell fellow, Ray. Big jeweler downtown with oodles of money. He's gonna get me an apartment n' everything, but I'm supposed to be white, see? I offered Janet the chance to be my maid, so she could stay with me, but she got all hincty and laid me low."

"Can't blame her, can you? After all she's been your best friend, and stuck by you through thick and thin. Doesn't it seem crass for you to want her to be your servant now that you've had a windfall?"

"Stuck by me?" she exclaimed angrily, seemingly unconscious that Raymond had said anything else. "You mean I've stuck by her. Didn't I get my mother to take her in when she had nowhere to go. in New York? Ain't I always been the one to hustle up money for us to live on? Stuck by me is good!"

"Calm down, sister. It's all oke by me. Have a drink?"

"Yes, thanks."

Raymond went into the alcove. A moment later he returned with two glasses, filled with cognac. "Here's to your new life, old dear. May it prove profitable, and may all your children escape the tar brush."

They sipped from their glasses.

"Think I'm doing right, Ray?"

"Why not? Doesn't it mean money? What else should you worry about?"

"Well, there's my family."

"Family? That is good. Pardon me while I laugh. Didn't your mother chase you out? Did she ever consider you when she passed for white?"

"I guess you're right, but. . . "

"But what? Tell me what's on your mind. It certainly isn't your family."

For a moment she stared into her glass. Raymond said nothing more. He sensed that something was preying on her mind, something about which she found it difficult to speak. He drained his glass and lit a cigarette. Finally she spoke.

"Well, Ray, I'll tell you. I'm afraid someone's gonna tell on me. This bloke doesn't know I'm colored, see? You know what happened to Mom. I can't have that happen to me. When I go white, I wanta stay white and never hear of being colored again."

"Which is just the proper attitude to have in order to be found out. Can't you people who cross the line understand that your own fears precipitate disclosure? The minute you leave the colored world, you live in unholy fear that Negroes you once knew might meet you somewhere and recognize you publicly. What if they do? Nine times out of ten that Negro is glad to see your change of status. You antagonize him only by ignoring him. Surely you've associated with enough white people around New York to know that most of them who happen to have colored friends make no effort to hide the fact. Why should you? Greet them as you would anyone else. Fail to do so and some of them are bound to talk, long and loud. Merely knowing a Negro does not necessarily stigmatize you."

"I s'pose you're right. Nevertheless, I kinda wish I was going to another town. I might get home sick for Harlem and come back."

"My dear, you've been reading novels. Thousands of

Negroes in real life cross the line every year and I assure you that few, if any, ever feel that fictional urge to rejoin their own kind. That sort of nostalgia is confined to novels. Negroes who can and do pass are so glad to get away they probably join the K. K. K. to uphold white supremacy."

"Well. . . I'm gonna do it anyhow. Just think, Ray. . . an apartment in the Fifties, a maid, fine parties, theaters and swell cafés. Ain't it gonna be grand?"

Raymond was not overly enthusiastic.

"I suppose it will. I'm sorry, Aline, but I've got to go out for a little while. Want another drink before you go?"

"Sure."

Raymond went into the alcove to pour out the drinks. While he was doing this Euphoria entered, followed by Paul. They both greeted Aline.

"Hello." She seemed uncomfortable, and the minute they went into the alcove to speak to Raymond, she quickly donned her hat and coat. As they emerged, she prepared to leave.

"Never mind the drink, Ray. I gotta go. See you."

She was gone.

"What's the matter with her?" Paul asked.

"A little nervous, I guess. She came to tell me she was crossing the line."

"Doing what?" Euphoria exclaimed.

"Going to pass for white."

"Bully for her," Paul approved.

"Why, the little hussy," Euphoria advanced indignantly. "Passing for white, eh? Just like her no account mother."

"Well. . . why not? I'm gonna quit being a nigger myself."

"What are you going to do, Paul, be born again?"

"No, Ray. I don't have to be born again. I can pass for Spanish. I have. Why, didn't I ever tell you about my trip to South America and how I was received at the Spanish Legation in Washington when I returned to this country?".

"Yes, Paul. I've heard that tale a million times. Can it. Take this drink. Here's one for you, too, Euphoria."

"No thanks. I don't want one."

"All the more for me. Here goes, Paul." They drained their glasses one gulp.

"Won't you even sit down, landlady mia?"

"No. I only have a minute and I've got something I must say to you. Where's Eustace?"

"Downstairs... isn't he, Paul?"

"Yes. Shall I call him?"

"Please."

Raymond and Paul exchanged quizzical glances. Something was most certainly amiss. Raymond shrugged his shoulders. Paul went to the head of the stairs and called Eustace. Euphoria lit a cigarette and paced the room, her eyes concentrated on the floor.

Paul returned to the room and poured himself another drink. Raymond seated himself in one of the wicker chairs, determined to be comfortable at all costs. Finally Eustace entered. He was much changed. True, he still retained in some measure his aristocratic bearing, but he was by no means as jaunty as he had been in the past. He seemed to be shriveling up, to be the victim of some inner dessication, which had left his exterior self without color or vitality. He still swathed himself in his green dressing gown, but the robin's egg ruby no longer adorned his index finger. It, too, had been sacrificed to alleviate economic stress, and now reposed in a pawnbroker's vault along with his other family heir looms, which, according to Eustace, had originated in Africa.

"You want to see me?" he inquired of no one in particular.

"Yes," Euphoria answered briskly, "I've got to have a talk with you all."

She stopped her pacing and leaned against the window casing. Eustace sank wearily to the daybed. Paul squatted on the floor in the center of the room and rested his back against the gateleg table.

"Pelham's going to be paroled within six months." She announced this startling bit of news with the air of a person ridding herself of some inconsequential trifle before settling down to the main event.

"Great," Raymond enthused. "I know he'll be glad."

"And he's finally come to his senses and decided to take up a respectable trade."

"Pray tell, what would that be?"

"He's going in for calcimining and painting, having had experience redecorating cell walls."

Raymond and Paul exploded, but were soon hushed by Euphoria's brisk continuance.

"That isn't, however, what I want to talk to you about. I'm going to change my policy about this house. You'll all have to move by the end of the month. That gives you three weeks."

"Move?" Paul repeated unbelievably. "What's the idea?"

Eustace continued to stare fixedly at the floor as if to say that one more bit of misfortune could not appreciably add to his discomfort. Raymond was too startled and nonplussed to speak.

"Yes. I mean it. I'm disappointed with this house. When I turned it into studios for you people, I thought I was filling a real need in the community. White artists downtown have hotels and houses where they live in a group, and I thought Negroes in Harlem should have the same type of place. I expected great things to come out of it. I expected it to contribute something to me and my talent, too. I was wrong. It's caused me nothing but worry, and given rise to nothing but slanderous gossip, which is detrimental to me as a businesswoman. I won't have people accusing me of running a miscegenated bawdy house any longer."

"Miscegenated bawdy house," Paul repeated merrily. "That is good." He began to laugh. "Ain't that a grand phrase, Ray?"

Raymond ignored him. It sickened him somewhat that Euphoria, the intensely vocal liberal, should allow local gossip to disturb her. And yet he realized that it was that and nothing more which had driven her to her present decision.

"Very good, Euphoria, I'll be glad to get out. I understand your position thoroughly." He spoke lightly, and hoped his tone had been sufficiently nonchalant, for he had no idea of letting her know how tragic the matter might really turn out to be. Where else in Harlem could he live comfortably, and as uninhibited, rent or no rent? To reside shabbily and conventionally in the usual Harlem rooming house, after these gloriously hectic months in Niggeratti Manor would be as detrimental to his wellbeing and work as would a penitentiary sentence.

Euphoria seemed pleased that her task was proving easy. She smiled at Raymond.

"I thought you'd understand," she said grate fully. "It's a matter of business, see? I must make money. That's all a Negro can do. Money means freedom. There's nothing to this art stuff. I've given up the idea of writing stories. I only want to make money."

"But what are you going to do with the house?" It was Paul who spoke. Eustace still stared into space, as if completely impervious to all that had been said.

"I'm gonna turn this house into a dormitory for Negro working girls between the ages of eighteen and thirty."

"Well, I'll be damned." Raymond was unable to suppress this.

Paul began laughing again. "You win the fur lined bathtub, old dear. Dormitory for working girls." He subsided into a fit of merriment.

"It isn't funny." Euphoria turned toward Paul and tried to quiet him with a steady glower. "It's something that has long been needed, a very serious enterprise. Where is there a place that's decent for young girls, young bachelor women rather, to stay? The Y. W. C. A. is a joke. Restrictions and whitewashed walls. No chance for girls to express their own personality. And these common ordinary room owning houses are not fit for decent girls to consider."

She looked around the room defiantly, silently daring anyone to contradict her. Paul continued to snicker. Even Raymond was beginning to be amused. Eustace alone remained oblivious to it all. Euphoria lit another cigarette, then began speaking again.

"Suppose Aline and Janet had had a nice con genial dormitory to move to when Aline's no good mother turned them out? Suppose Lucille had had such a place to live before she made her fatal misstep?"

She was prepared to say more, but was silenced by Paul's boisterous guffaws and Raymond's broad smile. She had, it seemed, said too much already. The saturation point had been reached. "Lucille's fatal misstep" was more than Raymond or Paul could bear. And they made no effort to restrain their mirth. Euphoria became indignant.

"I might have known you idiots would have no appreciation for a fine humanitarian enterprise. Should I open a gin mill now or encourage you to continue this. . . "

"Miscegenated bawdy house," Paul added mischievously.

She glared at him for a moment before continuing. "That's all I've got to say. You have three weeks to make other arrangements."

"What's gonna happen to the Pig Woman?" Paul inquired.

"She's going to stay and keep house."

"Ray for her," Paul waved his arms in the air. "And you, I suppose," he added maliciously, "are going to play Queen Sappho to this new Isle of Lesbos? I haven't been so thrilled since I first learned that Unconditional Surrender' Grant had a passion for horses."

Raymond could never clearly describe what happened during the next five minutes. He only knew that Paul, seated on the floor as he was, had been an astonished target for Euphoria's feet, and that his residence in Niggeratti Manor had ended then and there, despite the three weeks' notice.

XXIV

Raymond felt very much alone. It was amazing how in such a short time his group of friends had become separate entities, wrenched apart, scattered. Stephen up in Westchester County, tutoring the dunderheaded sons of a traction millionaire. Pelham in jail, dedicated to the proposition of finding an artistic outlet, calcimining cell corridors. Paul migrated to Greenwich Village after having been expelled from Niggeratti Manor for obscene *lèse majesté*, and so immured in the idiocies of another lunatic fringe that he had no time for subway trips to Harlem. Of Bull there had been no word at all. He had not been seen by anyone since his last interview with Lucille. Aline had crossed the line, and done it so successfully that there was no clue to where she had gone or what she was doing. Janet, too, had retreated to provinces unknown. It was rumored that she had become hostess in a cabaret in Newark, which catered to white trade only. Raymond had planned to investigate this report, but indolence had won. The trip from Harlem to Newark was tiring, even to contemplate. Janet remained unfound.

As for Eustace. Well, Eustace did not exist any longer. Even the shell had began to shrivel to a mere shadow of its former self. He had no spirit left, no vitality, no part of life. Nothing at all, except his love for afternoon tea and his persistency in singing Schubert's songs in a quavering, tired voice. He lived mechanically, animated only by a frugal stream of blood which his weary heart worked man fully to keep in action. Raymond had become so alarmed at his physical and mental apathy that he had called in a physician. As a result of this, Eustace had been forcibly carried to the city hospital, forcibly because he had no desire to live, and resented any artificial attempts to delay the end.

His unsuccessful audition had certainly been a stunning blow, one from which he would never recover. All of his life, the number of years were still a mystery, he had planned and studied, determined to become a figure on the American concert stage. The encouragement and acclaim he had earned from his uncritical Negro audiences had urged him on, given him confidence and an exaggerated conceit of his talent. Raymond had never been able to find out all that had happened at the audition. Eustace could not be persuaded to discuss the matter, and Samuel had not been near the house since Raymond had asked him to stay away.

And as for Barbara. It had been bruited about that the Negro doctor who was keeping her had for bid her coming to Harlem except to be with him. He had no desire to lose his treasure. So Barbara, too, was out of the picture. Raymond remained in Niggeratti Manor alone, he and the Pig Woman (the actress lady and her two daughters had moved shortly after Pelham's arraignment) and his loneliness was dissipated only by Lucille's too infrequent visits.

Once more Lucille had become, next to the novel on which he was now working, the most vital element in his life. Once more she had become his only companion, as had been the case when he had first met her soon after his arrival in New York. Aware of his depression, and also aware of the tremendous amount of energy he was pouring into his novel, she planned various theatrical dates, and arranged other diversions to provide him with intermittent hours of pleasure. She seemed to be privy to his every mood, and yet she never made herself a pest. Without her, Raymond, who so prided himself on being self-sufficient, admitted that he would surely have been lost.

On one particular night, when he had been unusually tired and moody, Lucille had called for him at dinner time, then produced tickets for a breezy musical comedy. And, after the theater, they had gone to their favorite Italian speakeasy where they had gorged themselves on spaghetti and Muscatel. Raymond, under the warming influence of the wine, had talked incessantly about his work. Lucille had been the perfect listener, subtly urging him to continue talking, feigning great interest in all he had to say, no matter how superficial and sophomoric it might sound to her. Finally, after having added two gin rickies to the wine, Raymond had suddenly become vocally cognizant of all she meant to him.

"'Cile, we ought to get married."

"Do you want another drink?"

"No, really, I'm serious."

"My dear Ray. Don't you realize that should we marry you'd probably cut my throat after the first week or else I'd bash you over the head with your typewriter?"

"But I love you."

"I don't doubt that. And I love you, too."

"At last?" His voice was joyous. His eyes sparkled with delight.

"Not at last, at all. I always have."

"But Bull. . . ?"

"Was an experiment I had to make."

Raymond studied her eyes for a moment before speaking again. "You're one queer girl."

"I assure you I'm quite aware of all my limitations."

"And you won't marry me?"

"I should say not. I happen to think too much, both of myself and you."

Once more Raymond grew pensive.

"Would you. . ."

"Be your mistress?" she finished as he paused. "Certainly." Then before he could give expression to his joy and surprise, she asked suddenly, and for no apparent reason. "Isn't that Ramona they're playing?"

Raymond had not even been aware of the sweet voiced tenor crooning over the radio.

"Why, yes it is," he answered after listening for a moment. "But what has that got to do. . . ?"

"It just reminds me of something. I think of it whenever I hear that song. You see it was like this," she smiled sweetly and leaned confidentially across the table, "I had a boyfriend. He was a butler to some wealthy white family. He took me to dinner one night and regaled me throughout the meal with the trouble his master had keeping a good cook. Finally fed up on it, I suggested that he marry and let his wife fill the position. The idea took hold. Immediately he proposed. And during his ecstatic outburst someone began singing Ramona."

"And the proposal?"

"Oh, he wasn't so keen after I told him I couldn't cook."

She began to laugh. Raymond did likewise. There seemed to be nothing else for him to do.

XXV

It was Raymond's last night in Niggeratti Manor. Lucille had spent most of the evening with him, aiding him to pack. The studio was bare and cheerless. The walls had been stripped of the colorful original drawings contributed by Paul and Carl Denny. They were now stark and bare. The bookshelves were empty, and yawned hideously in the more shaded corners. The middle of the room was filled with boxes in which his books had been packed, and in the alcove his trunk and suitcases stood at attention in military array. The rest of the house was also in a state of dishevelment. Painters and plasterers had been swarming over the place, leaving undeniable evidence of their presence and handiwork. Niggeratti Manor was almost ready to suffer its transition from a congenial home for Negro artists to a congenial dormitory for bachelor girls.

Amid the gloom and confusion Raymond and Stephen sat, fitfully conversing between frequent drinks which had little effect. There was more bad news. Stephen had been called back to Europe. His mother was dangerously ill. There was little hope of his arriving before she died, but they insisted that he, the eldest son, start for home immediately. He was to sail the next day.

"You know, son, family is a hell of a thing. They should all be dissolved. Of course I'm perturbed at the thought of my mother's death, but I can't stop her from dying, nor can I bring her back to life. should she be dead when I arrive. And yet I am dragged across an ocean, expected to display great grief and indulge in all the other tomfoolery human beings indulge themselves in when another human being dies. It's all tommyrot."

"Assuredly," Raymond agreed, "dying is an event, a perversely festive occasion, not so much for the deceased as for his so-called mourners. Let's forget it. You've got to adhere to the traditions of the clan to some degree. Let's drink to the day when a person's death will be the cue for a wild gin party rather than a signal for well-meant but purely exhibitionistic grief." He held his glass aloft. "Skip ze gutter." The glasses were drained.

"And after you get in Europe?"

"I will be prevailed upon to stay at home and become a respectable schoolmaster. Now, let's finish the bottle of gin. I've got to go. It's after three and As usual we've been talking for hours and said nothing."

Raymond measured out the remaining liquor.

"O. K., Steve. Here's to the fall of Niggeratti Manor and all within."

Stephen had gone. Raymond quickly prepared himself for bed, and was almost asleep when the telephone began to ring. He cursed, decided not to get up, and turned his face toward the wall. What fool could be calling at this hour of the morning? In the old days it might have been expected, but now Niggeratti Manor was no more. There nothing left of the old régime except reminiscences and gossip. The telephone continued to ring. Its blaring voice echoed throughout the empty house. Muttering to himself, Raymond finally left his bed, donned his bathrobe and mules, went out into the hallway, and angrily lifted the receiver:

"Hello," he grumbled.

A strange voice answered. "Hello. Is this Raymond Taylor?"

"It is."

"This is Artie Fletcher, Paul's roommate. Can you come down to my house right away? Something terrible has happened."

Raymond was now fully awake. The tone of horror in the voice at the other end of the wire both stimulated and frightened him. He had a vague, eerie premonition of impending tragedy.

"What is it? What's happened?" he queried impatiently.

"Paul's committed suicide."

Raymond almost dropped the receiver. Mechanically he obtained the address, assured Artie Fletcher that he would rush to the scene, and within a very few moments was dressed and on his way.

The subway ride was long and tedious. Only local trains were in operation, local trains which blundered along slowly, stopping at every station, droning noisily: Paul is dead. Paul is dead.

Had Paul the debonair, Paul the poseur, Paul the irresponsible romanticist, finally faced reality and seen himself and the world as they actually were? Or was this merely another act, the final stanza in his drama of beautiful gestures? It was consonant with his character, this committing suicide. He had employed every other conceivable means to make himself stand out from the mob. Wooed the unusual, cultivated artificiality, defied all conventions of dress and conduct. Now perhaps he had decided that there was nothing left for him to do except execute self-murder in some bizarre manner. Raymond found himself not so much interested in the fact that Paul was dead as he was in wanting to know how death had been accomplished. The train trundled along clamoring: What did he do? What did he do? Raymond deplored the fact that he had not had sufficient money to hire a taxi.

The train reached Christopher Street. Raymond rushed out of the subway to the street above. He hesitated a moment to get his bearings, repeated the directions he had been given over the telephone, and plunged into a maze of crisscross streets. As he neared his goal, a slender white youth fluttered toward him.

"Are you Raymond Taylor?"

"Yes."

"Come this way, please. I was watching for you."

Raymond followed his unknown companion into a malodorous, jerry-built tenement, and climbed four flights of creaky stairs to a rear room, lighted only by burning planks in the fireplace. There were several people in the room, all strangely hushed and pale. A chair was vacated for him near the fireplace.

No introductions were made. Raymond lit a cigarette to hide his nervousness. His guide, whom he presumed to be Artie Fletcher, told him the details of Paul's suicide.

Earlier that evening they had gone to a party. It had been a wild revel. There had been liquor and cocaine which everyone had taken in order to experience a new thrill. There had been many people at the party and it had been difficult to keep track of any one person. When the party had come to an end, Paul was nowhere to be found, and his roommate had come home alone.

An hour or so later, he had heard a commotion in the hallway. Several people were congregated outside the bathroom door, grumbling because they had been unable to gain admittance. The bathroom, it seemed, had been occupied for almost two hours and there was no response from within. Finally someone suggested breaking down the door. This had been done. No one had been prepared for the gruesome yet fascinating spectacle which met their eyes.

Paul had evidently come home before the end of the party. On arriving, he had locked himself in the bathroom, donned a crimson mandarin robe, wrapped his head in a batik scarf of his own designing, hung a group of his spirit portraits on the dingy calcimined wall, and carpeted the floor with sheets of paper detached from the notebook in which he had been writing his novel. He had then, it seemed, placed scented joss-sticks in the four corners of the room, lit them, climbed into the bathtub, turned on the water, then slashed his wrists with a highly ornamented Chinese dirk. When they found him, the bathtub had overflowed, and Paul lay crumpled at the bottom, a colorful, inanimate corpse in a crimson streaked tub.

What delightful publicity to precede the post humous publication of his novel, which novel, however, had been rendered illegible when the overflow of water had inundated the floor, and soaked. the sheets strewn over its surface. Paul had not foreseen the possible inundation, nor had he taken into consideration the impermanency of penciled transcriptions.

Artie Fletcher had salvaged as many of the sheets as possible. He handed the sodden mass to Raymond. Ironically enough, only the title sheet and the dedication page were completely legible. The book was entitled:

WU SING: THE GEISHA MAN

It had been dedicated:

TO
Huysmans' Des Esseintes and Oscar Wilde's
Oscar Wilde
Ecstatic Spirits with whom I Cohabit
And whose golden spores of decadent pollen.
I shall broadcast and fertilize
It is written.

Paul Arbian

Beneath this inscription, he had drawn a distorted, inky black skyscraper, modeled after Niggeratti Manor, and on which were focused an array of blindingly white beams of light. The foundation of this building was composed of crumbling stone. At first glance it could be ascertained that the skyscraper would soon crumple and fall, leaving the dominating white lights in full possession of the sky.

THE END

NOTE ABOUT THE AUTHOR

Wallace Thurman (1902—1934) was a Black novelist and figure of the Harlem Renaissance. Born in Salt Lake City, Thurman was a lifelong reader and writer who completed his first novel at ten and read the likes of Shakespeare, Havelock Ellis, and Charles Baudeliare. Moving to Harlem at the height of the Renaissance, Thurman had his hand in multiple literary productions such as *The Messenger*, *World Tomorrow*, and *Fire!!!*. A strong critic of the New Negro movement, Thurman found himself a part of the "Niggerati"—a group of Black artists and intellectuals who wanted to use their art to showcase African-American life as it authentically was whether good or bad—firmly against appealing to the Black middle class or the white gaze. Becoming one of the first Black readers at a major New York publishing house and experiencing prejudice on both sides of the color line, he felt moved to write *The Blacker the Berry: A Novel of Negro Life* (1929) and three years later, *Infants of the Spring*. Said by Langston Hughes to be, ". . . a strangely brilliant black boy, who had read everything and whose critical mind could find something wrong with everything he read," Thurman was a complex and important voice in the Harlem Renaissance.

bookfinity & MINT EDITIONS

Enjoy more of your favorite classics with Bookfinity,
a new search and discovery experience for readers.
With Bookfinity, you can discover more vintage
literature for your collection, find your Reader Type,
track books you've read or want to read,
and add reviews to your favorite books.
Visit www.bookfinity.com, and click on
Take the Quiz to get started.

Don't forget to follow us
@bookfinityofficial and @mint_editions

9 798888 970317